STRAW IN THE WIND

STRAW IN THE WIND

Mary Mackie

Chivers Press   •   G. K. Hall & Co.
Bath, Avon, England   Thorndike, Maine USA

This Large Print edition is published by Chivers Press, England, and by G.K. Hall & Co., USA.

Published in 1995 in the U.K. by arrangement with the author.

Published in 1995 in the U.S. by arrangement with Lawrence Pollinger, Ltd.

U.K. Hardcover ISBN 0–7451–2985–4 (Chivers Large Print)
U.K. Softcover   ISBN 0–7451–2999–4 (Camden Large Print)
U.S. Softcover   ISBN 0–8161–7453–9 (Nightingale Collection Edition)

The text of this Large Print edition is unabridged.
Other aspects of the book may vary from the original edition.

Set in 16 pt. New Times Roman.

Printed in Great Britain on acid-free paper.

British Library Cataloguing in Publication Data available

Library of Congress Cataloging-in-Publication Data

Mackie, Mary.
 Straw in the wind / Mary Mackie.
  p. cm.
 ISBN 0–8161–7453–9 (lg. print : sc)
 1. Large type books. I. Title.
[PR6063.A2454S77   1995]
823'.914—dc20   94–3345

CHAPTER ONE

I was always the odd one out—the youngest of four Ashborne children crammed into a three-bedroomed house on the outskirts of Sheffield. My two brothers and my sister were all energetic, good at sports, all dark-haired and exuberant in their different ways; I was small, fair, studious, preferring a good book to a game of tennis. Dad used to call me his little changeling and joke about my likeness to the milkman.

As, one by one, they left school at sixteen, my brothers and sister all took up varying careers—in the Navy, as a mechanic and as a shorthand typist. It was a surprise to them all when I opted to stay at school and become a teacher, but my parents gave me every encouragement.

Of course I had heard that young teachers were having trouble finding posts, but I hoped that the situation would have altered by the time I qualified. It didn't. For every vacant post there were twenty or more applicants. I tried everywhere, from Cornwall to Northumberland, but only twice did I succeed in gaining even an interview.

In desperation, because I hated being 'on the dole', I took a job as a receptionist to two doctors working in partnership, and that was almost a disaster, emotionally. I let myself become more than fond of the younger partner, and even dreamed that he might ditch his beautiful fiancée for me, but he remained oblivious to my secret passion. Shortly after he was married, he informed me, very kindly, that his wife was going to take over my duties. I left, with a slightly dented heart and a depressing certainty that I was never going to find permanent employment.

By that time, my oldest brother was married and living in Plymouth when he wasn't at sea; Ray, my second brother, had been promoted and moved to London; my sister, too, had married—her boss's son, who was an architect and had designed the fabulous house where they lived with their two small children. And poor old Jane, as usual, had to be different. I was twenty-three, out of work, a failure.

When the letter came, it gave no clue that its contents were to change my life, dramatically and irrevocably. It flopped onto the mat with a couple of bills for Dad, a postcard from Johnny in Hong Kong, and yet another 'Thank you but the post has been filled' for me. The letter in the blue envelope was addressed to Mum, postmarked Lincoln, and written in a hand I recognised as belonging to her old school-friend Muriel Ellis—'Muriel Farnsworth, as was', as Mum was wont to say. Muriel had joined the Army during the war, gained a commission and married a Brigadier

2

twenty years her senior, after which Mum had lost contact with her. Thirty years later, someone who knew them both had written to tell Mum that the Brigadier had died, so it was a letter of condolence which renewed the friendship and the correspondence had been going on for a year.

I put the blue envelope with the rest of the mail in its usual place in the lounge and swiftly forgot about it. My parents were both at work, so I was acting housekeeper, currently decorating the spare room because we hoped Johnny and his wife would come to visit when he returned from the Far East.

It must have been half-day closing because I remember that Mum came home at lunchtime from her work as assistant in a light-fittings shop. Still in my paint-spattered jeans and smock, with a scarf to protect my hair, I served poached eggs and baked beans and we sat discussing our different morning's activities. When I told her about the mail she said she would enjoy reading Muriel's letter later, when she had five minute's rest.

The landing was so crammed with furniture from the spare room that it was like an assault course as I squeezed past the wardrobe and upended bed. With the radio playing loudly in the empty cavern of the room, I lay on the floor painting the skirting board, enjoying the smells and the sunny yellow perfection of the walls. Johnny was bound to tease me about it.

3

Dreamy Jane doing the decorating?

I think I was singing along with the radio when Mum yelled from the doorway, 'No wonder you can't hear me with all this racket!' She turned off the radio and sat down on the step-stool in the middle of the room. 'I've been shouting at you.'

'Sorry.' I was concentrating on getting the top line of the skirting straight.

'Jane! Listen to me. You've been offered a job.'

I am rather proud of the fact that this amazing announcement did not make me splodge the paint up the wall as I sat up and stared in disbelief. 'A job?'

'Yes. Only a temporary one, I'm afraid, but it's all experience, and it is teaching.'

She was holding Muriel's letter so I assumed there must be a connection. Carefully laying the sticky paintbrush on the upturned lid of the paint tin, I got to my feet and wiped my hands on my jeans, excitement struggling with my scepticism.

'Where? When?'

'During the school holidays, she says.' She turned to the letter and began to quote, ' "Since his parents died so tragically, Gareth has been falling behind at school. I'm sure he could catch up with a little extra tuition, especially if he was in his home environment, and since your Jane is out of work perhaps she would not mind working during the summer" ... There!

4

She says you can stay in a cottage on the estate and help Gareth maybe two or three hours a day, or whatever arrangement is best. Well, he won't want to be doing school work all day every day during his holidays, will he? And you'll have plenty of free time. Lincoln's a lovely place to see, so they say. You can take my car. What do you think?'

My thoughts were too rapid and disjointed to recount. 'But I'm not a remedial teacher, Mum.'

'You don't have to be. There's nothing wrong with Gareth. He's just been too upset to concentrate, poor boy.'

'How old is he?'

'Almost fourteen. He's a bit of a loner, so Muriel says. Hasn't got any friends locally. He goes to boarding school. But I've told you all this before.'

'I know, but it's gone in one ear and out the other. I suppose you've told her all about us, too?'

'Of course! There's been a lot to catch up on.' She surveyed me thoughtfully. 'You don't sound very enthusiastic. I thought you'd be pleased.'

'I am, except ... it would be strange, teaching only one child, and in his own home.'

'But she's asking for your help. She's showing great faith in you when she hasn't even met you.' With a disapproving face she heaved herself off the stool. 'I'll leave you to

5

think about it. Come down when you've finished and we'll have a cup of tea. And Jane ... Muriel used to be my very best friend. It would mean a lot to me if we could help her. She's got her problems, you know, and now that she's lost her husband ... Well, I'll let you get on.'

Thinking dark thoughts about emotional blackmail, I prostrated myself once more on the floor and continued painting, though my mind was busy weighing up the desirability or otherwise of accepting Muriel Ellis's offer.

I was cleaning the paintbrush at the kitchen sink when Mum came from the garden with a bowlful of peas to be podded for dinner. She switched the kettle on and got out the tea-pot.

'Have you decided yet?'

'Not exactly,' I said. 'I mean, it sounds like easy money, but there must be snags. Suppose this Gareth is a little horror? How long ago did his parents die?'

'Oh, it must be a good two and a half years ago now. He'll be over the worst of his grief.'

'And he lives with Muriel—when he isn't at school?'

'That's right. Joel's his official guardian, of course, but they all live at Huntersmere.'

'Joel is ... Muriel's son?' I said slowly, dredging my memory.

I heard Mum sigh to herself as she was forced into repeating what I ought to have remembered. 'He's Johnny's age, or thereabouts. Muriel's got a daughter, too, called Serena, but she's married and has four-year-old twins, so she doesn't live at home any more.'

'Didn't you once say they were stinking rich?'

'The Brigadier was, from all accounts. Huntersmere's a biggish house with its own grounds, but they do run a market garden there. Oh, what difference does it make?'

'I'm just trying to build up a picture of what I shall be letting myself in for—if I go.'

Mum tutted to herself. 'All you'll be doing is helping a little boy with his lessons. The rest of the time you can suit yourself. With your own cottage, you won't have to get involved at all. If I was in your shoes, I should jump at it.'

I didn't exactly jump. I edged cautiously towards what I suspected might be a hidden minefield, beginning with a phone call to Huntersmere. Muriel Ellis sounded a charming woman, concerned about her grandson, anxious to help him in any way she could. Before I committed myself, she suggested, I might like to visit Huntersmere for the day, and since that sounded like a sensible idea, I agreed.

When we told Dad of the offer, he said I should take it. It would stop me being a drag on the tax-payer, if only for six weeks.

On a gloomy Saturday in mid-July, therefore, I set out for Lincoln in Mum's yellow Mini. It was a journey of less than a hundred miles, but complicated because it was cross-country. I had studied the route beforehand but still missed two turnings and then got stuck behind a huge lorry on a narrow stretch where it was impossible to pass. It was two hours before I had my first glimpse of the towers of Lincoln Cathedral standing high on the ridge. It was spot-lit by a lone shaft of sunlight which had found a gap in the dark clouds and I foolishly took it for a good omen. A few minutes later the heavens opened and the windscreen wipers had trouble clearing the view. The cathedral had disappeared behind the curtain of rain.

Weary and depressed, I stopped in the city for lunch before once more consulting my maps for the exact location of Delton-under-Edge. The rain had stopped by the time I reached the outskirts of Lincoln heading south under the Lincolnshire Edge and eventually turning into winding, narrow lanes which ran through numerous small villages and acres of farming land.

Delton itself was an attractive village of old houses and a few new bungalows centred round a church, a pub called 'The Black Bull', and a post office which sold a little of everything to judge from its crowded window. I pulled up to ask directions of an old man leaning on his garden gate and he pointed me towards Huntersmere. More and more I was wishing I had not come, but consoled myself that there was still time to find some excuse for refusing the job. Anyway, Muriel Ellis might not like me. My nerves were so bad that I had chewed my bottom lip raw.

Within seconds after leaving the village I was driving with the stone wall of Huntersmere estate on my left, while across the lane a field of young barley was still green, rippling in the wind that had sent away the rain. The sun sent a pale, diffused brightness through the thin clouds that remained.

I came suddenly upon the open gates. The park beyond was dotted with oaks and chestnut trees and the house was a formal Georgian edifice built of some stone that looked vaguely gold in the misty sunlight. A wide flight of steps ran up to a terrace; tall windows were set in symmetrical ranks. I tasted blood as I bit my lip again, for it was all much grander than I had imagined.

Leaving Mum's shabby little Mini at the foot of the wide sweep of stairs, I climbed to the front door and stood for a moment nervously smoothing my hair and straightening my blazer. But before I could reach for the bell the door was flung open and a fair-haired boy rushed out, looking over his shoulder so that he cannoned into me and for a moment we clutched at each other for support. Scarlet-faced, the boy looked up at me. He was dressed in jeans and a red sweater and had pale grey eyes that seemed oddly luminous.

'Gosh, sorry!' he gasped. 'I didn't see you. Are you Miss Ashburn?'

'Ash*borne*,' I corrected with a laugh. 'And you're Gareth, I assume?'

The end of the sentence was drowned by a roar from inside the house—'Gareth!' A young man dressed all in black, sweater and cords, came striding down the wide hallway, eyes blazing and face grim.

'I came to answer the door,' the boy lied, visibly shrinking away from the man's approach. 'This is Miss Ashburn.'

The man paused, looked me up and down, and ignored me. 'Gareth, you little beast, if I catch you in that garage once more...'

Gareth was cowering behind me, fearing the violence implied in the man's voice and manner and I immediately felt defensive. Whoever this stranger was, I disliked him on sight. He had dark hair and was deeply tanned, and in those black clothes he presented an impression of a dark personality, foul-tempered and ill-mannered, the whole lightened only by the flash of amazingly blue eyes.

Abruptly, he seemed to register my presence. 'You'd better come in, Miss Ashburn. My mother's waiting for you.'

His mother. So this must be Joel Ellis, Gareth's guardian. Poor Gareth.

As I stepped inside the hall, Joel Ellis reached behind me and grabbed the boy's arm, forcibly jerking him into the house and towards the stairs.

'Go up to your room and stay there,' he ordered. 'I'll be up in a minute.'

Gareth fled as if he were terrified and I glanced at his uncle, wondering exactly why he was so angry.

'I wish you joy of him,' he said darkly. 'Rather you than me. This way.'

The room to which he led me was large and well-proportioned, the graceful windows curtained in golden velvet. Small tables held an assortment of ornaments of porcelain, jade and onyx, and there were two huge bowls of yellow roses sending out their heavy scent. In the armchair by the fireplace, facing the door, sat a plump-faced woman whose dark hair was greying elegantly, curling softly round her cheeks. She wore an oatmeal dress over a turquoise silk blouse and at her lapel was pinned a simple gold brooch which had probably cost hundreds of pounds. She was reading a glossy magazine but looked up as we entered.

'Miss Ashburn is here,' her son announced.

'Ash*borne*, Joel,' she amended with a smile for me. 'My dear Jane, I'm so pleased to meet you at last.'

The sincerity in her voice made me relax a little as I crossed the thick carpet and shook hands with her, noting as I did so the two walking sticks propped by her chair, which explained why she had not risen.

'I'd have known you anywhere,' she informed me. 'You're exactly like your mother was when I knew her. Oh, so long ago! Sit down, my dear. Joel ... where is Gareth?'

'In his room,' he replied tersely. 'I found him messing about in my car.'

'Oh, dear,' Mrs Ellis sighed. 'I thought I heard an altercation. But he must meet Jane. Tell him to come down.'

'I will. But don't be surprised if he can't sit for a while.'

I perched on the edge of the settee, running my tongue over my sore lip and hoping the blood didn't show.

'Well, my dear,' Mrs Ellis said with a smile. 'How lovely it is to have you here. Ethel's daughter ... Oh, your mother and I had some high old times in the old days. I expect she's told you. I hope she's well?'

'Very well, thank you. She sent her love.'

'And you must give mine to her. You have no idea how much her letters have meant to me during this past year. So chatty and full of life. I'm hoping I can persuade her to spend a weekend here while you're with us—and your father, of course. We have so much news to catch up on. Over thirty years ... Do I gather you met my grandson?'

'We, er ... bumped into each other on the doorstep.'

'Ah.' Her smile made a dimple in one cheek.

'That sounds like Gareth. Always rushing somewhere. And Joel, I'm afraid, is rather protective over his car. Gareth loves anything mechanical. He'd like a motor-bike—to ride in the grounds, you know—but so far we have managed to put him off. They're such dangerous things.'

'Yes, they can be,' I agreed.

'Gareth's quite small for his age, as you probably noticed, but then his father was the same and *he* grew into a strapping six feet two. You know about David, of course?'

'David?' I said blankly.

'Gareth's father.'

'Oh—yes.' I felt my face flame. 'Yes, Mum did say. It must have been a . . . a terrible shock for you.'

She nodded her head sorrowfully, looking down at the hands that were twisted in her lap. Her knuckles were swollen with arthritis. 'Indeed it was. And then to lose my husband just over a year later . . . It's no wonder that Gareth has been unsettled. But that, of course, is where you come in. I'm hoping that besides giving him a refresher course you'll be able to bring him out a little. I feel he needs a younger woman, someone nearer his own age. He has Joel as a surrogate father, but I'm afraid the two of them don't hit it off. And my daughter Serena is busy with her own family. So Gareth has no one he can confide in. To be honest, Jane, I'm very much afraid that he may become

13

delinquent. Recently we've caught him lying—only about small things, but it may be the thin end of the wedge.' Pausing, she looked at me worriedly. 'Am I asking too much of you?'

'He may not even like me,' I said.

'That's true. But that's one reason I asked you to come today. I wanted to meet you myself, though of course I didn't know that Gareth would be here. He should be at school. Joel brought him home for the weekend a fortnight ago—it was my birthday and we had a family party—but unfortunately ...' She broke off, smiling brightly beyond me. 'There you are, Gareth. Come along in, dear.'

He trailed across the room with a red, rebellious countenance and I wondered if his uncle had carried out his threat to smack him. Vicious brute! I thought, surprising myself by the strength of my aversion to Joel Ellis, but then all my sympathy was with Gareth, the lonely orphan with the hurt eyes.

'You've already met Miss Ashborne, I hear,' Mrs Ellis said as the boy threw himself down in a chair.

Gareth flung me a glance under lowered lids. 'Yes.'

'Her mother is a very old friend of mine. We knew each other when we were even younger than you are. Jane's coming to spend the summer here and help you with your lessons.'

'I know,' he said sullenly.

'Well ...' She seemed at a loss. 'Would you

14

like to show her round the house? I'm sure she'd like to see the library, and your study.'

Without a word, Gareth stood up and looked at me expectantly.

'I'd love to,' I said. 'If you'll excuse us, Mrs Ellis.'

'We'll have some tea when you get back,' she called after us.

In the hall, Gareth pointed at doors, saying carelessly, 'Dining room, office, television room. Kitchen and stuff's at the back.' Sighing heavily, he stumped up the stairs, which had a sliding platform attached, presumably for Mrs Ellis's convenience.

There was a door at each end of the landing, and Gareth opened the one to the right, which gave onto a big rectangular library lined with book-cases, portraits, and a cabinet full of guns.

'The library,' he announced unnecessarily, padding across the varnished parquet floor to lean on one of the tables in the room.

My high-heeled sandals clumped on the bare parquet even when I went tip-toe. I felt like an intruder.

'You don't have to creep,' Gareth said. 'You should hear Joel walk across here. It's like an army in hob-nailed boots.'

Remembering Joel striding down the hall, I could imagine what he would sound like in the echoing library.

'Is he always that bad-tempered?' I asked.

15

The boy shrugged and turned away, moving on silent 'trainer' shoes to stare out of the window from where one could look out over the trees and see the distant cathedral standing sentinel over the wide vale.

'Did he hit you?' I asked.

'Not this time.' He swung round and sat on the windowsill, his lips curling a little. 'He's my guardian, you know. He thinks that gives him the right to push me around. He says my Dad would have done the same, but he wouldn't. I mean, heck, I only sat in his mouldy old car. Honest, you'd think it was made of gold, the fuss he makes about it.'

'But cars are very expensive,' I reasoned. 'Is it a new one?'

'He's had it a month. Only bought it to impress his stupid girl-friend.' He fixed me with narrowed eyes. 'I don't fancy doing lessons in the holidays. How boring!'

'It needn't be. If the weather's good we can work outside, if you like. Or take trips. It won't be like school. What's your favourite lesson?'

'Metalwork,' came the immediate answer.

'Oh, dear,' I said with a laugh. 'That's one thing I'm no good at, I'm afraid. I specialised in English.'

Gareth pulled an expressive face that demonstrated his revulsion. 'Ugh!'

'Don't you like English? Do you read much?'

'Not the rotten books they have at school.

16

Shakespeare. And poetry! Yuk! I'll show you what I like to read. Come on.'

Launching himself away from the windowsill, he hurried to a door in the far corner of the library. The room beyond had another marble fireplace, an assortment of armchairs grouped round a low table, several large cupboards—one of which was open to display an untidy pile of jigsaws—and everywhere there were plastic models of cars, ships and space vehicles. Gareth was opening one of the three further doors.

'This is my room,' he told me.

It was a large bedroom, well-equipped with bookshelves. A Monopoly board lay on the floor, with a game abandoned in the middle, the pieces and houses waiting for the next move, and a pile of Lego bricks was scattered nearby. Gareth stepped over them and picked up one of the motor-cycle magazines which were strewn across the bed.

'This is what I'm going to have when I'm old enough,' he said, turning to a picture of a powerful machine. He read me the specifications, glancing up with excited eyes to add, 'Top speed a hundred and fifty. Imagine that! Vroom! Like the wind.'

'My brother had one of those a few years ago,' I said.

'Did he? Did he let you ride it?'

'He took me on the pillion sometimes. I enjoyed it ... Who were you playing Monopoly with?'

'Myself. I often do. Nobody else likes it, except Irene. She'll sometimes have a game if she's not busy.'

'Irene?' I queried.

'Irene Reid. She's a sort of ... housekeeper. Do you like Monopoly?'

'Yes, I do. And I warn you—I usually win. My father says I was born lucky.'

A shadow passed over his grey eyes. 'Mrs Farrier's always saying, "It's better to be born lucky than rich." Maybe she's right. I'm not lucky.'

'Oh, yes you are,' I said stoutly, to cheer him up. 'You're going to have me here for the whole summer. We'll work, but we'll have fun, too. How's that for a bargain?'

He pretended to consider the proposition, but the lurking laughter could not be contained for long and he stuck out his hand with a grin. 'Shake on it.'

Almost without realising it, I had committed myself, but I liked the boy, sympathised with his loneliness, and wanted to help. I could think of worse ways to spend the summer.

Gareth jumped off the bed and went to kneel on the windowseat, beckoning me to follow. We looked from the rear of the house, across a cobbled yard flanked on two sides by stables. Beyond them the sun glinted on the glass of long greenhouses and off to one side there was an orchard. The middle distance was filled by a wood beyond which the tower of Delton church rose and there were glimpses of a few roofs and chimneys. As a backdrop to the view, the Edge rose steeply to the skyline, dotted with copses.

'That's where the cottage is,' Gareth told me, pointing. 'In the woods just near the church. In winter you can see the chimney from here. One of the gardeners used to live there until he retired. It's called ...' Hesitating, he glanced at the open door behind us and lowered his voice. 'They call it Peter's cottage. Only don't let Granny Muriel know you know. She gets very cross.'

'Oh?' I said cautiously, intrigued. 'Why?'

'I dunno. Some old scandal, Mrs Farrier says. Irene knows, but she won't tell. She calls it Peter's cottage, though, when nobody else is around. I'll take you there, if you like. They've had it all cleaned and aired for you. It's a pity you can't stay here, in the house. That'd be ace!'

'It would also complicate things,' I said. 'I'm to be an employee, not a guest. Anyway, I don't think I'd like to stay in the house.'

'Why not?'

'Because I don't know anyone. I'd feel ... uncomfortable.'

He clambered into a sitting position, hugging his knees, young face raised earnestly to mine.

'That isn't why they're putting you in the
19

cottage,' he informed me in the tones of one imparting a dark secret. 'Granny Muriel was planning to have you in the house, only Joel put his foot down. They had an awful row about it. I was in the conservatory and I heard them. First he didn't want you to come at all—he said it was a waste of money. And then he said, "If you're determined to do it, let her use the cottage. I'm damned if I'm having some nosey female snooping around. When she isn't earning her money I want her out of here." That's what he said.'

'Nosey female?' I repeated, insulted. 'He hadn't even met me.'

'No, but ...' His gaze suddenly swung beyond me and he jumped visibly. I turned to see a tall, thin woman standing in the doorway. She wore a plain cotton dress and flat, soft shoes, and her brown hair was done in tight curls which didn't suit her long face.

Gareth gave a groan of relief. 'Oh, it's you, Irene.'

'Thank your lucky stars for that,' she returned briskly. 'It could have been Joel. If he'd heard you telling tales ... You'd better come down at once. Your grandmother is waiting for you.'

'This is Miss Ashborne,' he said, taking a flying leap from the windowseat to the bed.

'So I gathered. How do you do, Miss Ashborne. I'm Irene Reid. Mrs Ellis is waiting and the tea's made. Don't let it get stewed.'

As she turned to leave I noticed the way her left arm hung, limp and useless, making her move a little awkwardly. It must hamper her duties as housekeeper, I thought, but despite her brusque manner I suspected that she, too, felt sorry for Gareth. Perhaps the entire household disapproved of the way Joel Ellis treated his ward, though since he was legal guardian there was probably little they could do about it.

But why, I wondered, had Joel been so adamant about my staying out of the house? What was he trying to hide?

CHAPTER TWO

When I arrived home that evening, Mum was anxious to hear all about Muriel Ellis and Huntersmere. Over a fish and chip supper, I recounted the story of my day.

'She did say she had arthritis,' Mum interrupted, 'but she didn't say it was that bad. Poor Muriel. And what about the cottage? Is it nice?'

'Not bad. Two up, two down, and a shower room added onto the kitchen. They let it out to holiday visitors last year, apparently, but it wasn't very successful. It's not really a holiday area. The furniture's a bit shabby, but it will do for my purposes. Oh, and Mrs Ellis said to tell you that she hopes you and Dad will go and spend a weekend at Huntersmere during the summer.'

Mum looked at Dad, who wasn't enthusiastic but said that they might be able to fit it in.

'It sounds a bit grand for my taste,' he added.

'Muriel's not grand!' Mum objected. 'Don't you remember...'

'I remember a skinny kid in pigtails. Now she's the wealthy widow of a Brigadier, living in a mansion. You might be disillusioned, Et. She's climbed way above us. Besides, what would I do all weekend, with the two of you gossiping?'

'You can always come to the cottage,' I laughed. 'And you'd be interested in the market garden. Maybe you could persuade Joel to show you round.'

At that Mum came out of her plans for the weekend—she had probably been doing a mental inventory of her wardrobe. 'Did you meet Joel? What's he like?'

'I only saw him briefly, but don't get any ideas in that direction, Mum. He's a bully. Gareth doesn't like him, either. Even Mrs Ellis said the two of them don't get on. And he doesn't approve of my going there. He resents his mother spending the money and he thinks I'm going to poke my nose in. So I shall stay well clear of him. If I see too much of him I might be tempted to tell him what I think of him. But I shall try to keep Gareth out of his way, too. That boy needs love and attention, not the heavy hand.'

'If I were you,' Dad advised, 'I wouldn't get too involved, Janie. It's their own business how they bring the boy up. You don't want to be accused of interfering.'

'I don't intend to interfere, only give Gareth a happy holiday for once. And how involved can I get in six weeks?'

'Up to your neck, if you're not careful,' he said. 'It'll probably be a good idea if we do come over—to see what you're getting up to.'

His warning amused me. I was sure my intentions were innocent enough and no harm would come of them.

*   *   *

Early the following Saturday morning, I left home with the Mini crammed with clothes, books and provisions, plus a few ornaments and personal bits to make the cottage more homely. The weather was good and the cathedral towers seemed to welcome me, though this time I drove straight through the city and on into the flat vale beyond.

In Delton, I turned down the narrow lane between the low-walled churchyard and the long garden of the 'Black Bull'. Fifty yards ahead I could see the gateway, which was the

23

back entrance to Huntersmere, framing the curving road which ran through the woods towards the house. The cottage stood to the right, just beyond the gateway.

I was driving slowly to pass the shallow ford which guarded the gate, and my caution proved lucky, for as the car nosed between the gateposts a pony and rider suddenly burst from the woods in front of me, apparently heading for the gate. I slammed on the brake as the pony reared in fright, its hooves only inches from the bonnet, and the rider fell. It all happened in seconds, but it was long enough for me to recognise Gareth.

As I leapt out of the car there was another rush of hooves and motion and a larger horse erupted from among the trees, with Joel Ellis sliding from the saddle even before it halted. He jerked the horse to a stop with a firm hand as he bent over the prostrate boy. But before his uncle's hand could touch him, Gareth rolled away, coming to his knees to glare at Joel furiously from beneath the peak of his riding hat.

'Don't touch me! You meant that to happen!'

'Damn it, Gareth!' Joel said breathlessly, again reaching for his nephew.

This time the boy slapped the hand away. 'You did! You know Dusty gets nervous. You meant me to fall!'

Joel stared at him, then straightened himself,

saying grimly, 'Don't talk like an idiot. Are you hurt?'

'No. No thanks to you.'

For a moment Joel seemed lost for words, then he suddenly rounded on me accusingly. 'Don't you know better than to career down country roads?'

I suppose I gaped like a stranded fish, astounded by the unwarranted attack. 'I was practically stationary! Anyway, he must have heard the engine.'

'Of course I did.' Gareth was on his feet, soothing the nervous pony. 'It wasn't your fault, Miss Ashborne. Dusty was out of control—because you frightened him, Joel. You know you did.'

Joel sent me an exasperated glance before turning his back on me. His voice revealed that he was controlling his temper only with difficulty. 'Are you sure you're not hurt? Can you ride back?'

'I expect so,' came the reply. 'I'm just a bit wobbly. You don't have to wait around. I'll come when I'm ready.'

'We'll go together,' Joel said through clenched teeth, a muscle working in the corner of his jaw. It was difficult to tell with whom he was more angry—Gareth for his accusations or me for being a witness to the incident. 'Gareth, get in that saddle before I take my belt to you.'

The boy glanced at him, face ugly with hate.

'You wouldn't dare!'

'Try me!' He took a step towards Gareth, who dodged round the pony, fumbling for the stirrup. With a jerky movement he swung up to the saddle, dug in his heels and edged the pony past my car, heading towards the village at a fast trot.

I heard Joel let out his breath as he reached for the reins of his own mount, flung a leg across it and checked, glancing down at me as if he felt impelled to say something. 'My nephew is very highly strung. Good morning, Miss Ashburn.'

Seething, I watched as he rode in pursuit of Gareth. I disliked that man sufficiently to wonder how much justification there had been for Gareth's accusations. But what possible reason could Joel have for wishing to harm his own nephew?

When they were out of sight I drove on towards the big house, emerging from the woods and driving past the greenhouses, where two vans emblazoned 'Huntersmere Market Gardens' were parked. I pulled into the stable yard at the back of the house and as I climbed from the car Irene Reid appeared at the kitchen door, to pick her way daintily across the cobbles, her paralysed arm supported by her other hand.

'You'll be wanting this, I expect,' she said, handing me the cottage keys. 'Mrs Ellis says if there's anything you need you have only to ask.

She will expect you promptly at nine o'clock on Monday morning.'

'I'll be here,' I promised, though I was aware that I was being politely told to keep away until it was time to begin my duties.

As she moved away, I noticed another woman peering round the kitchen door, with an elderly man in the shadows behind her. They were probably Mrs Farrier, the cook, and Partridge, the butler, of whom Gareth had told me. No doubt they wanted to get a look at this new addition to the staff.

It took me some time to unpack the Mini and make the cottage tidy again before deciding what I should have for lunch. With my own things around me and my radio playing I felt more at home, but I was bothered by what had happened earlier. It had looked as though Joel was chasing Gareth. Had the boy been misbehaving again? I remembered his face, livid white beneath the black hat, ravaged by a mixture of anger, pain and—yes, and fear. I had clearly gained the impression that he was afraid of his uncle, though he had tried to cover it with a show of bravado.

Puzzling over the incident, I was sitting in the kitchen with a cup of coffee when I heard the front door open and Gareth call, 'Hello? Miss Ashborne?'

'In here,' I replied. 'Hello, Gareth. What...'

He indicated the Monopoly box under his arm and grinned, though it seemed to me that

27

the grin was a little forced. 'I've come to take you up on that challenge.'

'Already? I've hardly finished my lunch.'

'I'll help you wash up. You weren't going out, were you? It's clouding over. The forecast said it would rain this afternoon.'

'Did it? Well, I had thought I might take a look at the Cathedral, but if it's going to be wet ... Okay, set it up in the other room.'

By the time I had cleared the table he had the board spread out on the floor of the front room, the money and cards in neat piles near it. I took one of the saggy cushions from the settee and put it on the floor as a seat.

'You've recovered from your accident, I see,' I said.

Gareth looked at me blankly. 'Accident?'

'You fell off your pony!'

'Oh, that. Yes, I'm all right, thank you. Grazed my elbow a bit, that's all.' He looked at the dice jiggling in his hand. 'It *was* Joel's fault, you know.'

'Was it?'

'Shouting and yelling ... He made Dusty bolt.'

'What was he shouting and yelling for?'

'Oh, *I* don't know,' Gareth said wearily. 'There's always something. He's really got it in for me, Miss Ashborne ... Do I have to keep calling you Miss Ashborne?'

'Well ... no, I suppose not. My name's Jane.'

He grinned—properly this time. 'I know.

28

Okay, Jane. Double six to start?'

We soon became engrossed in the game, buying property and putting up houses. Outside the clouds gathered and the wind rose to bluster through the trees, soon to be joined by the soft sibilance of raindrops. For once the weather forecast had been accurate.

I was confined to jail and practically bankrupt, Monopolywise, when I heard a car coming from the direction of Huntersmere. The throaty roar of the engine snarled to a halt at the cottage gate, making Gareth look up in alarm.

'It's Joel!'

'Maybe he's looking for you,' I said, getting stiffly to my feet. I could see Joel climbing from a low red sports car.

'Tell him I'm not here!' Gareth gasped, and dived behind an armchair.

With a face as dour as the clouds overhead, Joel Ellis strode hurriedly up the path, reaching the door as I opened it. He barged straight in without waiting for an invitation and stood brushing raindrops off the sleeves of a blue sweater.

'Where is he? Ah, there you are! And what do you think you're playing at? I told you to stay at home this afternoon.'

Reluctantly coming out of his unsuccessful hiding place, Gareth stood up and faced his uncle sulkily. 'I am at home. I didn't leave the grounds.'

29

'You know damn well what I meant!' Joel shouted, his movement making the boy flinch as if he expected to be struck. 'It's lucky for you that you told Irene where you were going. If I'd had to come searching for you ... And your bike's out in the rain. Can't you take care of anything?'

'I forgot,' Gareth said.

'Forgot? You just don't give a damn, that's your trouble. All you care about is your own pleasure. You'll defy me one time too many, my lad.'

Gareth had been growing redder in the face, as if holding the lid on his emotions. Now the tears burst from his eyes and he yelled, 'What will you do then? Kill me?'

Unable to listen to any more, I rushed to put my arm protectively round the boy's shoulders and turned to say something that died on my lips as I saw the expression on Joel's face. He looked sick, as if someone had struck him, and all the colour had gone from his face.

'Really ...' I began uncertainly, not understanding the emotions which lay beneath this scene. 'He hasn't been doing anything wrong. I'm sorry about the bike. I didn't realise...'

'Go and get in the car,' Joel ordered in a taut undertone. 'Do you hear me, Gareth? You can come and get your bike tomorrow.'

Gareth stepped away from me, drying his face with his sweater sleeve, and took a wide

30

detour round his uncle to reach the door, while Joel stared grimly at the game on the floor. He didn't look up until Gareth had gone.

'You're being employed as a teacher, not a nanny,' he said, his voice low with disgust. 'Two or three hours a day, Monday to Friday, was what was agreed, I believe. That's all you'll be paid for, Miss Ashburn.'

For a moment I was speechless, astounded by what he was implying, then my temper came to my aid. The man was a bully and a cynic and it was about time he discovered I wasn't a doormat.

'That's all I expect. But I assume I'm free to do as I like with my spare time, even if I choose to spend it with your nephew, Mr Ellison.'

His frown deepened. 'It's Ellis,' he said coldly.

'And *my* name is Ash*borne*. And if Gareth likes to come here he can do so, as often as he likes. It might give him a rest from being your whipping boy!'

For two seconds of singing silence, we glared at each other.

'If I were paying your wages,' he said, 'you'd be on your way right now. What has Gareth been telling you?'

'He didn't need to tell me anything. I can see for myself. He's terrified of you.'

'So you've already assigned us our roles, have you? The poor helpless orphan and the wicked guardian? Well, perhaps when you grow up you'll realise that life is seldom quite that black and white.' He turned on his heel and opened the door. 'I'll put Gareth's bike in your out-house for now.'

He left the door wide open, the rain splashing in. As I closed it forcibly I saw him wheeling away a blue racing cycle. 'When you grow up ...'? The man was insufferable!

*　　　*　　　*

I was roused early the next morning by what sounded like a thousand birds praising the glory of the sunrise. I tried to go back to sleep but eventually gave up the struggle and went to open the sash window and lean out to smell the freshness after the rain. The sky was an unsullied blue, the sun just lifting over the church tower, glinting on the miriad raindrops among the leaves in the wood. A perfect morning, I thought, leaning happily on the windowsill.

'But soft!' quoted a disembodied male voice from somewhere below me, 'what light through yonder window breaks? It is the East, and Juliet is the sun.'

Startled, I half-withdrew from the window, scanning the trees and shrubs round the cottage, but I could see no one. I must have been light-headed, drunk on the morning dew, for another line from the same scene of 'Romeo and Juliet' popped into my mind and I found myself saying it aloud: 'How cam'st thou hither, tell me, and wherefore?'

There was a rich chuckle and a young man stepped from behind the screening branches of the hawthorn bush by the ford. 'The only other bit I can remember is "A horse, a horse, my kingdom for a horse." And that's not even from the same play. Maybe it should be "my kingdom for a ladder", under the circumstances. What on earth are you doing there?'

'I might ask you the same,' I said. 'You gave me a fright.'

'Not half as big a fright as you gave me. I'm walking my dog, minding my own business, and suddenly the window of a deserted cottage shoots up. I thought it was the ghost.'

He had an engaging grin and a pleasant face capped by floppy brown hair. Jeans and a T-shirt with some legend I couldn't read clothed a lanky frame now half-hidden by the hedge round the cottage garden.

'Ghost?' I said.

'Oh, it's only a local folk-tale. Nothing to worry about ... I thought they'd stopped renting the cottage out to visitors.'

'Did you?'

'You have rented it, I assume? You're not a squatter?'

'Do I look like a squatter?'

'No. Actually you look like something out of my favourite dream. What's your name?'

33

'Jane Ashborne. And you?'

'Ray Prentiss, spinster of this parish.'

'I've got a brother called Ray,' I told him.

'Have you? He's not with you, is he?'

'Good heavens, no!'

'You're alone?' Noting my hesitation, he added swiftly, 'I didn't mean it that way. I'm not a would-be rapist. It just seems odd that a girl like you should be holidaying alone out here in the back of beyond.'

'Did I say I was holidaying?'

He looked puzzled. 'But if you're not ... then what *are* you doing here? Don't tell me you're the new head gardener?'

'No, I'm not,' I laughed. 'Don't be so nosey.' A shiver ran through me and I rubbed my arms. 'It's not very warm yet. You'll have to excuse me.'

'Wait! Don't disappear like that. Have a drink with me at lunch-time. Just down the road at the "Bull". I'll meet you there about half eleven. Okay?'

'I'll think about it,' I said, and closed the window laughing to myself.

Having taken a shower, I put on jeans and a blouse and made myself some breakfast, reading a book as I ate to chase away the feeling of loneliness; then the sun drew me out into the garden, which was a wilderness of weeds and rosebushes running amok.

As the church bell began to call people for morning service, I checked the out-house to

34

make sure Gareth's bike was still there. The brick building appeared to have been a coal-shed, for there was still a black tide-mark up the wall and across the floor, with the expensive bike looking out of place. I was closing the door when a car went past, only its black roof visible above the hedge.

Just over an hour later, the same black car drew up at my gate and disgorged an unfamiliar Gareth, dressed in a grey suit, his hair shining and neatly combed. The car drove off again, but not before I had glimpsed Mrs Ellis in the back.

'Good morning,' I hailed the boy from the doorway. 'Have you been to church?'

'She makes me go,' Gareth grumbled, kicking viciously at a stone with his highly-polished shoes. 'I've come to get my bike.'

'Would you like a glass of squash?'

'Yes, please. Only I can't stay long. I've had orders.'

'From Joel?'

He nodded glumly and followed me through to the kitchen. 'It's not fair. You didn't mind me coming yesterday, did you? Joel said I was making a nuisance of myself. Just because *he* thinks I'm a nuisance...'

'Well, he's wrong. You can come whenever you like—unless you'll get into trouble for it. Did your grandmother say anything about it?'

'No. I don't think he told her.'

I was relieved to hear it. 'Thank goodness!

I'm afraid I was rather rude to him yesterday.'

'Were you?' His eyes sparked with interest above the glass of lemon squash. 'Why, what did you say?'

'I lost my temper. I shouldn't have done. But he was being so ... boorish. There's a good word for you. Look it up in the dictionary when you get home.'

'Mrs Farrier says he's like a bear with a sore head,' Gareth informed me.

'Does she? Well, she may be right, but I'm not sure we ought to talk about your uncle this way. He probably has things on his mind that we don't understand. And you do like to try his patience, don't you?'

'He gets on my wick!' Gareth said. 'Always ordering me about. Always sending me to my room if I even breathe too loud. He hates me!'

'Oh ... Gareth, that's a very strong word.'

'He hates me, I tell you! And I hate him. When I'm eighteen ... he'll be sorry. He'll be very sorry. And he knows it. That's why ...' He hesitated, looking down at the empty glass in his hand and adding in an undertone, 'He'd like to get rid of me.'

'Get rid?' I queried in a low voice.

He flung back his head and I saw the fear in his eyes. 'Kill me! He would!'

'Gareth!'

'It's true! But he won't get away with it. I've written it all down in a book. About the swing, and about the poison ... You saw what happened yesterday, with the pony. I've put that down, too, so if something else happens they'll know! They'll know it was him who did it.' He put down the glass and darted to open the back door.

'Gareth!' Alarmed, I went after him and stood in the doorway of the shed as he grabbed his bike. 'Gareth, it can't be true. You mustn't think such things. He may be impatient, but he wouldn't ... He's your uncle!'

He swung the bike round so that the front tyre was pointing at me. 'He's not. He's only my half-uncle. And he ... he killed my father. Or somebody did. There was no reason for that 'plane to crash. I heard them say so.'

'You probably heard wrong. You're imagining all this. I know you don't like your uncle, but ...'

'I'll have to go,' he said. 'Please get out of the way. He'll come after me if I'm much longer, and I don't like being alone with him.'

Worried, I moved aside and walked with him to the front gate. 'Have you told anyone else about this?'

'They wouldn't believe me. *You* don't believe me ... Hold the bike a minute, will you?'

I did so, while he bent and tucked his trousers into his socks to keep them from flapping on the chain. I didn't know what to say. What did he mean about the swing and poison?

37

'Gareth...'

'I must go,' he said, wrenching the bike from my hands. ''Bye, Jane. And don't you worry about me. I'm ready for him. He'll have a hard job getting rid of *me*.'

'Just you be careful!' I called after him.

Of course it was all nonsense. Gareth was an imaginative boy and his parents' death had obviously affected him more than I had realised. What possible motive did he imagine Joel would have for attempting murder? Joel was short-tempered and bad at dealing with children, but that didn't mean he was a criminal.

Deep in thought, I walked slowly back to the cottage, but as my hand touched the doorknob a voice from the gate hailed me and I turned to see my 'Romeo' of the dawn smiling at me.

'Eleven thirty,' he said, displaying his watch. 'Are you coming? Don't tell me you'd forgotten.' Opening the gate, he ambled down the path and stood before me, head on one side. 'Something wrong?'

'No, not really,' I denied. 'Is it half past eleven already?'

'It is. And you look as though you could use a drink. Was that Gareth Ellis I saw riding away?'

'Yes, it was.'

'In with the folks at the big house, are you?'

'He left his bike here.'

'O-oh? Curiouser and curiouser, said Alice. I

shall investigate further over a couple of pints.'

'I might tell you to mind your own business!' I retorted. 'Wait here while I fetch my handbag.'

When I returned he was by the gate with an old golden labrador beside him. The dog padded slowly after us as we leapt across the ford and walked on down the lane.

'Do you live in Delton?' I enquired.

'My parents run the shop. They moved here twenty-five years ago, when I was two. That explains me. Now what about you. Where are you from?'

'Sheffield.'

'Ah, yes. Steel foundries and industrial smog.'

'It's not like that at all. Anyway, we live on the outskirts.'

We decided to stay in the pub garden rather than face a smokey bar on such a lovely day. Leaving me to find a seat, Ray went to get the drinks. The garden was pleasant, rough tables and benches set under the trees, and to one side a few swings and a slide which several small children were using to good effect while their parents relaxed. I discovered a small vacant bench beneath a lilac tree and sat down, watching two older boys swing like monkeys on tyres strung by thick ropes from the branches of a chestnut tree. The labrador flopped beside me.

'I wish I'd brought my camera,' Ray said as

he returned with a pint for himself and a lager for me. 'You make a super picture sitting there, except I'd prefer a happier face. You look as though you've got the worries of the world on your shoulders.'

'I was just thinking.'

'About what?'

'Things. What do you do—apart from making charming speeches to strange women?'

'I work in Lincoln. In an office. What about you?'

'I'm a teacher. At least, that's what I trained for, but until now I haven't been able to find a job.'

'Until now?'

'Mrs Ellis hired me to help her grandson do a bit of cramming.'

His eyes opened wide. They were dark brown, friendly eyes. 'So that's the explanation. And she's relegated you to the cottage?'

'Hardly relegated. It suits everybody better.'

'Yeah, I'll bet!'

'What does that mean?'

'It means you'd better watch out for Joel Ellis. He's the local Casanova. Always a new girl. If I were you, I'd make sure I locked my doors securely at night.'

'I always do. And I can't see Joel trying to seduce me, of all people. I'm way beneath his notice. Besides, it was a case of mutual dislike at first sight.'

Ray considered his beer thoughtfully. 'They, er ... they say that he and his nephew don't get on too well, either.'

'Really?' I said cautiously, unwilling to gossip about the Ellises' private affairs.

'There's been some talk. Mrs Farrier—she works at Huntersmere—lives next door to us. She says there's always trouble between those two. Gareth goes out of his way to annoy Joel, and Joel is quick to respond. There was a bit of aggro between Joel and David, too. David was Gareth's father.'

'Yes, I know.'

'There was bound to be trouble, I suppose, with all that money going to the Figgins side of the family. They say the Brigadier put himself in hock keeping the place going for David, and now history's repeating itself.'

'I'm not sure I follow you,' I said, puzzled.

'No? It's a long story and I don't intend to bore you with it. Suffice to say that when David and Angela were killed, Gareth became the heir. When he comes of age the whole place, plus the Figgins fortune, will be his. And Joel will be left out in the cold.'

I stared at him, not believing my ears. Was that what Gareth had meant? 'When I'm eighteen, he'll be sorry,' he had said. 'That's why he'd like to get rid of me.'

And there was a motive after all; one of the oldest motives in the world—money.

CHAPTER THREE

'Talk of the devil,' Ray interrupted my whirling thoughts, bringing me back to the sunlit garden, the happy sound of children playing.

'Sorry?'

'That was Joel Ellis just went past. Didn't you hear the car?'

'Oh—yes.' The echo of the snarl of a powerful engine was still on the edge of my hearing.

'Taking the latest girl-friend home for Sunday lunch, no doubt,' Ray guessed. 'It beats me how he does it—unless he makes believe that *he's* the heir-apparent. Or is he frantically attractive, from a woman's point of view?'

'He's not bad-looking,' I granted. 'Ray ... what did you mean about "the Figgins side of the family"? Aren't they all Ellises?'

'They are now. Look, if I'm going to tell you the tale I need another pint. Drink up. Do you fancy some sandwiches?'

'Aren't you expected home for lunch?'

'Not necessarily. Mum opens the shop Sunday mornings, so we have dinner at night. I told her I might not be in. Beef or ham?'

'Beef, please.'

Left alone again, I watched a tiny girl totter

past clutching a bag of crisps which were scattering across the grass, but my mind was back at Huntersmere. Just because there was an inheritance involved didn't mean that Gareth's tale of attempted murder was true. It was so melodramatic. And Joel didn't strike me as the calculating type. He was more likely to lash out in a fury than to play the cold waiting game. But then what did I really know about him? I had met him—or, more precisely, encountered him—all of three brief times.

'So what were we talking about before we were so rudely interrupted?' Ray asked as he resumed his seat beside me. 'Ah yes—the local gentry. At least, they like to think they're gentry, though the blue blood's got a bit watered down recently.'

'You were going to tell me about the Figgins,' I reminded him.

'Figginses,' he corrected. 'Not that I remember them. They were before my time. But I've been sufficiently interested to find out ... It all began with a Figgins way back, who made a fortune out of the tea trade. Josiah, I think his name was. Anyway, he built Huntersmere and the family continued. Politics and property, etcetera. By the time Sir George arrived on the scene there was still a considerable fortune left. That's Sir George Figgins, eighteen fifty-seven to nineteen forty. His tomb's in the churchyard. He outlived all his children and his only grandson, so he left

43

everything to his granddaughter Elizabeth, who was born and raised at Huntersmere. She's in the churchyard, too. If you like, we could have a wander over there when we've finished.'

'I'm intrigued,' I said. 'What happened to the heiress?'

'Oh, that's quite a tale in itself. Back before the war—while Sir George was still alive—Elizabeth started to kick over the traces. They say she was only seventeen when she ran off with a carpenter who was here to do some renovation work on the church. Of course her grandfather put a stop to that, brought her back and married her off to Brigadier Ellis.'

'*The* Brigadier Ellis? Muriel's husband?'

'That's right. I shouldn't think he was a Brigadier then, but he was a lot older than Elizabeth. Probably Sir George thought he would be a steadying influence. And from that union came David Ellis. Old Sir George lived long enough to see his grandson and from all accounts he was contented to have a male heir, after Elizabeth. What he couldn't have foreseen was that Elizabeth herself would die only two years later. She was only twenty-two, according to the dates on her stone.'

'And she left everything to a two-year-old baby?'

'Apparently so, though the Brigadier had use of the house for his lifetime. He had money of his own, anyway. When the war ended, he

44

married the present Mrs Ellis, and along came Joel and Serena, with no claim to the Figgins inheritance.'

'I see. Ray ... exactly what happened to David and his wife?'

'They were killed in a 'plane crash. He was piloting his own executive jet and it smashed into a hillside, in Snowdonia, I think. They were brought back and buried here with appropriate pomp and ceremony. I *do* remember that. The whole village was in a state of shock for days afterwards, and the Brigadier had a stroke. He survived for eighteen months and then *he* died, though at least he'd had more than his threescore years and ten ... Drink up and let's have another, then we'll go for a romantic stroll round the churchyard.'

The graves were all there, as he had told me—the huge stone tomb of Sir George Figgins; the marble slab for his granddaughter Elizabeth; the double grave of Gareth's parents, and the newly-set stone of Brigadier Ellis. I understood now why Gareth had called Joel his half-uncle. David and Joel had had the same father, but different mothers.

Ray walked me back to the cottage and would have stayed if I had given him the least encouragement, but I told him I had to prepare for my first lessons with Gareth, so he went away saying that he would 'see me soon'. It wasn't that I didn't like him, but I was aware of how isolated the cottage was and to have invited in a young man I hardly knew might have been asking for trouble. Besides, I had a lot to think about.

What Ray had told me was local gossip—the 'aggro' between Joel and David; the antipathy between Joel and Gareth; the 'plane crash ... plus the swing and the poison which Gareth had mentioned. Not to mention the incident with the pony.

Sitting on the threadbare settee, I tried to remember every detail of that near-collision in the gateway. It had all happened so quickly. I remembered the pony rearing, Gareth sawing at the reins, then ... Since I had been leaping out of the car at the time, it was all impressions and not clear memory, but it seemed to me that Gareth had landed on his feet. Yet when Joel appeared, the boy had been lying on the ground, apparently dazed. But he had moved quickly enough when Joel went to help him.

It was no good. I couldn't remember with any accuracy and I was no longer sure what was memory and what was imagination.

'I wouldn't get too involved, Janie,' Dad had said, but getting involved was exactly what I was doing. I must remember that my only function here was to help Gareth with his schoolwork, not poke my nose in ... The phrase struck a chord. Joel hadn't wanted me in the house because he was afraid I might pry. What was he afraid I might find out?

At that moment I heard the unmistakable

46

roar of Joel's car coming down the road. To my horror it stopped at my gate and I heard the door slam. It was as if my thoughts had reached out to warn him of my suspicions and bring him hurrying to inflict his wrath on me.

When I opened the door, he met me with a worried stare. 'Miss Ashburn—borne. I'm sorry to trouble you. I was here earlier. You were out.'

'Yes, I ... had lunch out. Is something wrong?'

'Yes ... No ... I mean, I'm not sure.' He ran a hand through his hair as if trying to pull himself together.

'You'd better come in,' I said, concerned. He was so unlike his usual self. 'Whatever's happened? It's not ... Gareth?'

'Yes, I'm afraid it is Gareth. He had a nasty fall off his bike, just after he left here this morning. Cut his lip and took the skin off his hands and his leg ... You didn't touch the bike at all, did you?'

'No, of course not. But how is Gareth? Will he be all right?'

'The doctor says so. The thing is ... it looks as though someone disconnected the brake cables, and it can only have been done overnight, when the bike was here. It was fine when he rode it yesterday.'

I stared at him in horror until it dawned on me what he was suggesting. 'You surely don't think that I ...'

47

'No, naturally I don't!' he snapped.

'But you had to ask! That bike hadn't been moved. I looked this morning to make sure it was still there, but it hasn't been touched since you ...' My voice trailed off.

'Since *I* put it in the out-house, you mean?' Joel finished for me, an unpleasant glint in his eyes. 'But I didn't touch the brake cables. I didn't have the time, did I?'

I shook my head, hardly noticing that I was backing away from him. 'I don't know. How long would it take?'

'Oh, for God's sake!' It was a cry of anguish. He sat down suddenly, on the arm of the settee, and spread his hands on his knees. 'The shed doesn't lock, does it? Anyone could have got in and ... were you with Gareth when he took the bike out? You didn't leave him alone, even for a few seconds?'

'What ... Oh, you're not suggesting that he did it himself? That's crazy. It's wicked!'

'I wouldn't put it past him ... No, he wouldn't go that far ... You see, I don't even know what I do think, except that I'm pretty sure I shall go out of my mind if this doesn't stop.' Both hands went to his head, kneading the tumble of dark hair. 'Did you hear anything in the night? Any sound outside?'

'No. But during the evening I had the radio going pretty loudly, so ...'

He looked up, leaping on the thin hope. 'So someone might have got into the shed without

48

your hearing anything?'

'It's possible, but … Mr Ellis, *why* should anyone do such a thing?'

'I don't know,' he said with a gesture of helplessness. 'I just don't know. None of it makes any sense. But whoever it was, it wasn't me. Whatever you think of me, at least believe that. I do get angry with Gareth. I admit that. But I wouldn't hurt him. Do you believe me?'

'Of course.'

A derisive gleam came into his blue eyes. 'Thank you for saying it, even if you aren't sure.'

'I really don't know anything about it,' I protested.

'Of course you don't. I'm sorry I asked. I'm sorry I dragged you into it. Maybe I was clutching at straws. I hoped you would say you had heard something.' Sighing heavily, he let himself slide from the settee arm onto the cushions, as if he were tired out. 'Mother told me not to come. She said the idea of intruders might frighten you. If that's so, I apologise. But if you're afraid to stay here you can come up to Huntersmere. Mother would like that.'

He looked and sounded as if all the energy, all the desire to fight, had left him.

'When I was young,' he said, resting his head on the back of the settee, 'I used to come here with Sam Wilkins—he was head gardener. It always smelled of fresh baking. Mrs Wilkins made the best bread I ever tasted. Crusty, and still warm from the oven, so that the butter melted ... God, that seems like another life.'

'Well, I can't offer you fresh-baked bread, but if you'd like a cup of tea, or coffee...'

'No.' He sat up straight, giving me a taut smile that failed to dispel the weariness in his eyes. 'Thank you, but I've taken up enough of your time. I must get back. I've left a young lady making small-talk with mother, and neither of them are very pleased with me.' With another deep sigh he heaved himself upright, straightening his jacket. 'I'm sorry I was so unpleasant to you yesterday. I was ... uptight.'

'I know you were. And I ... shouldn't have said ... what I said.'

'Call it quits?'

'If you like.'

'I like. I've got enough enemies without adding you to the list.' He opened the door, but paused on the path outside. 'Thanks again. Goodbye, Miss Ashborne—burn.'

'You were right the first time,' I said, unable to suppress a smile. 'Ashborne. With an "e".'

Joel shook his head ruefully. 'Now I'm thoroughly confused. Will you settle for Jane?'

'It's easier to remember, anyway. Will Gareth be feeling up to lessons tomorrow?'

'I should think so. It will give him something to occupy his mind. If not ... you can always finish that game of Monopoly that some unfeeling brute broke up yesterday. See you tomorrow, then.'

50

'Yes,' I said, and closed the door wondering why my heart-beat was so unsteady. My bottom lip was sore again. Was I afraid of Joel Ellis?

I saw him now in a different light—as a man harrassed almost beyond bearing—unless he was a very good actor. If he had meddled with the bike, it might suit him to make a fuss about it, to throw suspicion away from himself. It had been his choice to leave the bike unprotected in my shed.

It occurred to me that Ray had been in that vicinity, very early in the morning. But anyone in the village would have had the same opportunity—if he had known the bike was there. Yes, that was the salient point. Who could have known that Gareth's cycle was in my out-house, apart from Gareth, myself— and Joel, of course. It all came back to Joel.

And if he was really so worried, why hadn't he called the police?

With that thought in mind, I was disconcerted when, early that evening, a young constable came to ask the same questions as Joel had asked. Patiently, gravely, he looked at the shed.

'Are you going to take fingerprints?' I asked.

'No, I don't think so, love. I only came because Mr Ellis insisted. I've seen the bike. The cables could easily have come loose and just given way today. The lad doesn't take much care of it, if you ask me. Front tyre's

51

nearly worn through with skidding. You know what kids are like.'

'So you think it was an accident?'

'Can't see any other logical answer. I mean, it would be such a daft thing for anybody to do on purpose.'

I tried hard to believe him, but it was yet another peculiar 'accident' to add to the growing list.

On Monday morning I parked the Mini in the stable yard at Huntersmere and carried my heavy briefcase and the Monopoly box into the kitchen, where a shirt-sleeved Partridge was stacking crockery into an ancient dish-washer. He looked round in surprise.

'Morning, miss. I think you were expected at the front.'

'Was I? Oh, I'm sorry, I thought I wouldn't bother everyone. How's Gareth this morning?'

'He looks like a prize-fighter, but he's chirpy enough. Children bounce back quickly, not like us old folk.'

Despite his white hair he was still active, trim. His eyes were bright in his wrinkled face and as he talked about 'old folk' he smiled, as if he knew he was in excellent shape for his age.

'You'd better go up,' he added. 'Can you find the way?'

'Yes, I think so. Are there any back stairs?'

'There are, but they aren't safe at the moment. Dry rot. We're waiting for the builders to put it right. But you're not a servant, you know. I think Mrs Ellis would prefer it if you used the front door in future.'

He was politely telling me that I was trespassing in his domain, so I apologised and promised not to come through the kitchen again.

As I crossed the hall, I heard Mrs Ellis call from behind a partly-open door to my right, 'Is that you, Irene?'

Pausing, I pushed the door further open so that I could see her sitting in a wheel-chair at a bureau. Sunlight streamed into the room through two tall windows.

'No,' I said. 'It's me. Good morning.'

'Jane, my dear. Good morning.' She turned the chair to face me. 'Sorry about this, but my silly arthritis is bad today. I didn't hear the door-bell.'

I stepped further into the room and set my briefcase on the floor. 'I'm afraid I came the back way. Your butler isn't very pleased with me.'

'Partridge is an old fuss-pot. He was here when Sir George Figgins was alive, and in those days one was expected to observe all the niceties. He rather disapproves of our casual ways, to tell you the truth ... I was hoping to see you. How are you getting on at the cottage?'

'It's fine, thank you.'

A frown briefly creased her forehead. 'You've had a rather more eventful beginning than I might have wished. I do apologise for all that bother yesterday. Really it was too silly of Joel to make such a fuss. He was worried, of course, but he needn't have made it ten times worse. The whole thing was Gareth's own fault. The policeman said that the brakes had been loose for some time.'

'Yes, so he told me.'

'So you see, there was no intruder, no one creeping around the cottage in the night. Joel didn't frighten you with that absurd story, I hope?'

'Not at all. I slept like a log.'

'I'm glad to hear it. But if you are at all nervous there's a room here you can use.'

'Thank you, but I'm very comfortable at the cottage. Please don't worry about it.'

'The offer will stay open. If anything should … disturb you, just let me know.'

'Thank you,' I said again, but her insistence puzzled me. Was she expecting something alarming to happen at the cottage?

'Then I won't delay you any longer. Gareth is in his room, I believe. Shall I send your love to your mother? I'm writing to extend a definite invitation for them to come. "An offer they can't refuse", as they say.' She smiled at her own joke. 'You'll lunch with us, of course … Now, Jane, I'll take no arguments. Naturally you will lunch with us. You're a friend of the family.'

Murmuring my thanks, I picked up the

book-filled briefcase and departed.

I was wearing flat walking shoes that morning and the soles squeaked on the library floor as I walked to one of the big tables and put down my briefcase and the Monopoly box. As I did so, a paper aeroplane came sailing through the air, skidded across the table top and fell to the floor. Gareth grinned at me from the doorway to the ante-room, though the grin was lop-sided because one side of his mouth was swollen, and as he came towards me I saw the deep cut in his top lip.

'You're late,' he told me.

'I was talking to your grandmother. How are you?'

'All right, I suppose. It hurts a bit when I talk. You know what happened?'

'Yes, I know.' I scanned his face worriedly. He looked pale and battered. 'You should really take more care of your bike.'

His grey eyes filled with disgust. 'You're like the others. They say it was an accident, too. But those brakes were okay on Saturday. They were okay until *he* got at them.'

'You can't be sure of that, Gareth. Anyway, let's not discuss it now. We've got work to do. Have you any school books I could see?'

'Oh, flippin' heck!' he muttered, and stumped away.

I emptied my briefcase of its contents— books, notepaper, pen and pencils, and arranged them on the table. Gareth came back with a handful of exercise books and several brand-new text books.

'Granny Muriel got them,' he explained with a glower. 'Do we have to study? I've got a terrible headache... Hey, you packed away the game! Now we shall never know who won.'

'Yes, we shall. I wrote everything down, so we can carry on where we left off. Now that's enough side-tracking.'

He slumped into a big leather armchair, holding his head and making a melodrama of the supposed headache, but he brightened when I showed him the teenage novel I had bought for him. It concerned the exploits of a youngster who was leader of a motor-cycle club. He was much misunderstood by his elders but triumphed in the end by helping to solve a robbery. I had scoured the bookshops in Sheffield for hours to find such a book and since its cover showed the group astride their motor-cycles it appealed immediately to Gareth.

'Shall I read it now?' he asked.

'You can make a start, while I familiarise myself with the work you've been doing.'

There was silence in the library. Gareth had both elbows on the end of the table, his fair head bent over the novel, while I sat with my back to the window, going through his books and making notes. He was fairly good at maths, though there seemed to be some problem with equations, and for most of the

56

other subjects his marks were good to average. I wondered what Mrs Ellis was worried about until I saw that occasionally he had gained very low marks, mainly because of carelessness, brevity and illegible handwriting.

'What's "intrepid"?' he asked, looking up from the book.

I passed him a dictionary. 'Look it up. And write it down, with its definition.'

'Oh, Jane!' he groaned.

'It's the best way to fix it in your head. And don't scribble. Remember somebody else may want to read it.'

'Yes, Miss Ashborne,' he said, pulling a face, but he did as he was told.

I didn't hear the door open, but heavy footsteps on the bare floor made me look up. Seeing us, Joel paused and came on more quietly. He was dressed for work, in jeans and a grey flannel shirt, the sleeves rolled up to display tanned, muscular forearms.

'Good morning. Hard at it? Is he behaving?'

I glanced at Gareth, who was absorbed in his book. 'I think we shall make progress.'

'"Boorish",' Gareth said to himself, reaching for the dictionary. 'A ... B ... Here it is—"Boor, noun: Peasant; clumsy or ill-bred fellow. Hence, boorish." Shall I put that down, too?'

'Yes, please.'

'What on earth is he reading?' Joel said.

'Oh, that's not in the book,' his nephew

informed him, writing in his notebook. 'Jane said it yesterday. She told me to look it up. We were talking about you at the time, Joel.'

Joel's eyes met mine and I felt myself flush hotly. Until then I had forgotten I had used the wretched word.

'I'm so pleased to have been useful in widening Gareth's vocabulary,' Joel said levelly, though his eyes sparked blue fire. 'Excuse me for interrupting the valuable lesson,' and he strode away towards the door in the corner, his shoes pounding on the floor.

When the silence resumed, Gareth was engrossed in his book again.

'That was unnecessary, Gareth,' I said in a low voice.

He glanced up, face guileless, eyes innocent. 'What was?'

'You know what was! You were very rude to your uncle.'

'*I* was? But I only...'

'You only repeated what I said. Yes, quite. But you knew what you were doing. Or were you trying to get me into trouble?'

His face went blank, as if he had not thought of that aspect of the matter, but before he could say anything Joel returned, in a blazing rage.

'Gareth!' he roared as he burst into the library. 'Have you been in my room?'

'What?' said Gareth, looking startled.

'Have you been in my room?' Joel repeated, stopping a few feet from his nephew, restraining himself with a visible effort. 'Well?!'

Gareth shook his head violently, shrinking deeper into the chair. 'N-no! Honest, Joel!'

'Then who has?'

'Irene made the beds.'

'Irene wouldn't open my bureau!' Joel shouted.

'Well, it wasn't me!' Gareth yelled back.

I leapt to my feet, my head buzzing. 'Please! Do we have to have a screaming match? Mr Ellis ... how can Gareth and I be expected to work with these constant interruptions? If he says he hasn't been in your room...'

'He'd say anything that suited him,' Joel said roughly. 'Very well, I'll let you be. But I shan't forget this, Gareth, and if I find anything missing, God help you!' He turned away, moving with long, rapid, noisy steps to the far door.

I caught Gareth thumbing his nose and sticking his tongue out after his uncle.

'That's enough!' I snapped, my nerves worn thin. 'Put your book away now. We'll have a session on equations.'

My brusqueness surprised him, but it also had the desired effect of making him behave.

Some time later, Partridge brought a tray of coffee and biscuits for us and I allowed Gareth a break. I was tired myself, for there was some point about equations that he was failing to understand and I couldn't discover which exact point it was. I was beginning to wonder if

59

the fault lay with him or with me, for I was not a specialist maths teacher.

'I shall have to go to the loo,' Gareth announced.

'Go ahead. Where is the bathroom?'

'The door next to mine. The other door's Joel's room.' He stood up, adding significantly, 'I lock my door at night, so he can't get in. 'Scuse me.'

Sighing to myself, I went to lean on the windowsill, looking out at the cathedral. It must have been nearly ten miles away but its outline was clear against the blue sky, pale in the sunlight. I might have considered myself lucky to be in such pleasant surroundings if it had not been for the undercurrents that surged around me, dragging me first one way and then another. Was Joel an evil man, or was he not? Had there been murder attempts, or were they accidents?

Not your business! I told myself sharply, and turned back to the table.

As I went to pick up the coffee-pot, I noticed the paper aeroplane still lying on the floor. I bent to retrieve it, seeing that it was made of pink paper with writing on it. Idly, I opened it out and began to read.

It was the last page of a passionate love letter. There was something about 'nights that seem endless when I don't see you', and 'if only I could hear your voice, darling Joel'. I barely glanced at it after I realised that it was private, but I did see that it was signed 'Helena' and ended with a row of kisses.

My immediate reaction was embarrassment. I wondered if Helena was the girl Joel had brought home for Sunday lunch. But as I instinctively folded the page another thought struck me and I became still, a chill shiver running through me. The letter belonged to Joel yet Gareth had been in possession of it. He must have been in Joel's room. He had lied about it, blatantly, the young monster.

And if that was so, how many other lies had he told?

CHAPTER FOUR

Lunch was due at one o'clock but was delayed because Joel was late. When he did arrive he said that one of the vans had refused to start. He still had traces of oil on his hands.

'I could have fixed it,' Gareth boasted.

'Thank you,' Joel replied, 'but I fixed it myself, without having to call in an expert. What have you been doing?'

'Equations,' Gareth said glumly. 'I'm hopeless at them.'

We discussed his problem and to my surprise Joel said that he would see if he could help. After that the conversation turned to the market garden and I learned that they grew all manner of salad and other vegetables, plus some soft fruit. The cellars were given to mushroom cultivation. Several local hotels and restaurants were regular customers.

All the time I was aware of the folded page of the letter. I had put it in my shirt pocket and wondered that everyone did not notice the square outline. I had not mentioned it to Gareth. After long consideration I had decided to tackle the problem another way.

Joel excused himself as soon as he had finished and I knew that I, too, should take my leave. Gareth wanted to come with me, but Mrs Ellis reminded him that his aunt and cousins were coming for the afternoon.

'Why don't you stay and meet them, Jane?' she added.

'I've already intruded long enough,' I said, edging towards the door. 'Thank you very much for the lunch. I'll see you tomorrow,' and I escaped before she could press me.

I let myself out by the front door and walked to the end of the terrace, where a ramp led down to ground-level along the eastern end of the house. Passing the entrance to the stable-yard, I came onto the grass verges which surrounded the greenhouses. A peach tree was trained, under glass, against the wall of the stables facing south, and a path led beside it, emerging from between walls of glass into the wide cultivated area where vegetables grew.

There was a man hoeing between the kidney

beans at the far side of the garden, while closer at hand a youth was pulling peas, his bare shoulders tanned to a golden brown.

'Is Mr Ellis around?' I asked.

'In the far house,' he replied, pointing down the long line of sun-glinting glass.

There were three huge greenhouses, set end to end, containing cucumbers, aubergines, peppers, lettuce, radish ... Dad would love to see them, I thought. He was very proud of what he produced from our own garden and small greenhouse.

The far house appeared to be empty apart from the spreading foliage of the tomato plants. It was hot and humid in there, making me sweat.

'Mr Ellis?' I called.

Joel stood up in the middle of the jungle and stared at me in surprise. 'What are you doing here?'

'May I talk to you for a minute?'

'Is it important? I'm busy.'

'I can see that, but ... Yes, it is important.'

'Oh, very well. Come down this middle path. And bring some of those wire supports, will you?'

Looking round, I discovered the thin wire rings in a plastic punnet, so I took them with me as I edged down the gravel path, being careful not to catch the delicate plants.

'Thanks.' Joel was on one knee, rubbing out the side shoots and securing the branches to a

63

complicated framework of canes. 'Hold the box, will you? Well, what is it?'

'It's about Gareth.'

He glanced up at me bleakly. 'Is it ever about anything else? What's he done now?'

'Nothing. At least, it's not so much what he's done as...'

Silently, he held out his hand, palm upwards, which I assumed meant that he wanted one of the rings. I gave it to him and he used it to fasten a drooping branch that was heavy with young fruit. 'Go on. I'm listening.'

'This morning...' I said awkwardly, wishing I didn't have to talk to the back of his head. 'This morning...'

'Get on with it!'

'I'm trying to! But it's not easy with half your mind on something else. I ought to have known better than to try and talk to you. You're not really interested, are you? Why you ever took on the responsibility...'

He leapt to his feet, towering over me grim-faced. 'I keep wondering that myself. It isn't as if I hadn't got enough on my plate already. Of course I'm interested, you stupid woman! Vitally interested. But it's also vital to keep these plants in good order. This time of year it's difficult to keep pace with them. And when I've finished here I've got a pile of paper-work to get through. But go ahead. You have my full, unswerving attention.'

'I can't possibly talk to you while you're in

this mood,' I said, thrusting the punnet at him. 'Here, hold it yourself. I'm employed as a teacher—part-time—not a gardener's mate.'

He opened his mouth to reply, but a small voice from the door forestalled him, calling loudly, 'Uncle Doel! Yoo-hoo, uncle Doel!'

Joel shut his eyes tightly, counted to five under his breath, and answered with forced pleasantry, 'Hello, Philip.'

There was a giggle and a little boy of perhaps four years old appeared at the end of the path.

'Oh, God, our help in ages past,' Joel muttered to himself. 'Philip ... stay there. Where's your Mummy?'

'I'm here.' She was in the doorway, a lovely brunette with long curling hair. 'He ran on ahead. Didn't you, monkey?' As she claimed the child's hand I saw that on her other side she held a small girl, a replica of Philip except that she was wearing a dress and not short trousers. 'It's all right, Joel, they won't hurt the plants. Run off to the house, children. Go and find Gran and Gareth.'

The twins obeyed, fighting to be the first through the door, while their mother came on down the path between the tomatoes, smiling rather archly.

'This is Miss Ashborne, with an "e",' Joel said, as though it was important to establish my identity right away. 'My sister Serena.'

Laughing, Serena held out her hand. 'It's Jane, isn't it? Lovely to meet you. For a moment I thought you were a new notch on Joel's hunting knife. When I saw you in here I was wild with curiosity. He doesn't usually expect his girls to get their hands dirty. What on earth *are* you doing here?'

'We were trying to have a quiet talk,' Joel said with ill-concealed impatience.

'In a *greenhouse*?' Her eyes widened with amusement, as blue as Joel's but fringed with long lashes that I suspected were fake. Still, they suited her.

'We thought it would be private,' Joel said, 'but obviously we were mistaken.'

'Obviously. And what, exactly, was so private? You aren't trying to charm Jane into your net, I hope? You and I, Jane, must have a long talk about this brother of mine.'

'Yes, do that!' Joel exclaimed. 'Only go somewhere else and do it, will you? Some people have work to do.'

'H'm,' his sister mused, one finger tapping her lips thoughtfully. 'The famous charm *is* wearing a bit thin lately. What's wrong, Joel? Middle-age creeping up on you? They do say thirty is an awkward age.'

'It's not my age; it's my blasted family! I never get a minute's peace.'

Serena arched a perfect eyebrow at me. 'It looks as though we both chose the wrong moment. Shall we retreat and wait until the master's in a better mood?'

'It might be as well,' I said, and followed her

66

to the door.

But before we left she could not resist another jibe at Joel—'The heat does affect some men adversely,' to which Joel replied, 'Get lost, Rena!'

It was a relief to be in the open air, where it felt quite cool after the humidity of the greenhouse, not to mention the heat of Joel's temper.

'Where are you headed?' Serena asked.

'My car's in the yard. I was on my way back to the cottage. If I'd had any sense I would have gone straight there instead of bothering your brother when he's busy.'

'Bothering him about what?'

'Oh ... just something to do with Gareth's lessons,' I lied.

We paused beside the blue estate car she had left in the road, and Serena sighed. 'I shouldn't pull Joel's leg, I suppose. He's not really that bad. In fact, as brothers go he's rather special. I wish I knew what's eating him. You mustn't think he's always such a bad-tempered bear. Time was when he'd have been delighted to see me—and the twins. They adore their "uncle Doel", but even they are beginning to realise he's not himself any more. They can't understand why he never never wants to play with them. Still ...' She gave me a sad little smile. 'I mustn't bore you with our family problems. I hope I'll see you again soon, Jane. 'Bye for now.'

When she had driven on, I followed on foot to the stable yard, the page from the letter feeling like a brand against my skin. What had I hoped to accomplish by talking to Joel, anyway? I could expect only impatience and anger, not the calm, reasoned discussion which the problem warranted. It remained only to hope that he would forget about the whole thing.

I spent the rest of the afternoon and part of the evening in the cottage garden, removing weeds while I moped, thinking about Gareth and Joel. I wished that I could discuss the problem with my parents, for they might have been able to advise me. Since Gareth had lied over one thing, was it right to assume he would lie over other things? Had he lied out of sheer fear of Joel? But why had he ever gone into Joel's room at all? He must have known the risk he was taking. Did he enjoy making Joel angry?

And as for Joel himself, both his mother and his sister had said that his impatience was of recent origin. What had caused it? What was 'eating him'? The fact that Gareth would inherit Huntersmere in four years time?

'I thought you said you weren't the new gardener,' Ray's voice said from the gateway. 'Hi! Coming for a drink?'

'In this state?' I sat back on my heels, displaying my hands.

'Nothing to stop you washing your hands

68

first. I'll wait.'

'Thanks, but no thanks. Not tonight, Ray. I'm going to take a shower and have an early night when I've finished this patch.'

The gate clicked as he came through it. 'I was afraid you might find Gareth Ellis a difficult pupil. Getting you down, is he?'

'What makes you think that?'

'The way you looked before you saw me. Here, let me give you a hand.' He caught my elbow and helped me rise. 'Stiff?'

'A bit,' I admitted, stretching my aching legs. 'But a hot shower will put that right.'

'And then you can put something feminine on and come for a drink. Just a nightcap. You don't want to go to bed yet. It's barely nine o'clock.'

I almost refused, but the prospect was inviting and after a day with the Ellises I was in need of some congenial company.

'Yes, why not? But you're going to have to wait in the front room and behave yourself.'

'But naturally. What else would I do?'

He remained in the front room with the door closed while I took a shower and then slipped upstairs to do my face and put on a summer dress. Ray declared that the wait had been well worthwhile and we walked down the lane chatting.

Although it was almost dark by that time, there were still people sitting in the garden at the 'Bull', enjoying the mild evening. The bar

69

was crowded, every seat taken and at least a dozen people standing, but after a while two seats became vacant and we grabbed them, Ray on a stool and myself at the end of a padded bench.

'I hear the lovely Serena was visiting Huntersmere this afternoon,' Ray said. 'Mum saw her go past with the twins. Did you meet her?'

'Briefly.'

'Gorgeous, isn't she?' He looked rueful. 'I had a powerful yen for her at one time, but she never so much as glanced my way. She was in the year ahead of me at school. Boys wilted at her feet even then.'

'She was at ordinary school?'

'Oh, yes. It's only Gareth who's been sent away. David and Angela liked the social life too much to have a child around all the time. No, David, Joel and Serena went to school locally. The two boys went on to University. Serena wasn't quite that bright. All she ever thought about was horses. I can see her now, riding through the village on a fat pony, long pigtails bobbing ... It was no surprise to anyone when she married Alan Maine.'

'Who's Alan Maine?' I asked. 'I mean— apart from being Serena's husband.'

'He owns the riding stables. He's quite a bit older than Serena. Everyone assumed he was a confirmed bachelor until he started courting her. Mind you, he was in with David before

70

that. Went into partnership. Bought lots of new equipment, horses ... There was talk of them starting a stud, but nothing ever came of it. Alan seemed to lose interest when David was killed—or more likely he lost his main source of capital. From all accounts David was a bit of a fool about money.'

'You do know a lot about them, don't you?' I said.

Ray laughed. 'If you live in this village you can't help but know a lot about the Ellises. They're our own home-grown Forsyte Saga. There's little enough else to talk about in Delton. And it's catching. You're interested, too, aren't you?'

'I suppose I am. More than I should be. My father warned me not to get involved.'

'You can hardly avoid that, working there. Tell me about your day. Was Gareth a brat?'

'No worse than usual. He's a mixed-up boy, that's all, spoiled in some ways and deprived in others. I'm having a hard time understanding him.'

'In what way, particularly?'

'In every way.'

There were some things, I thought, that the village had no right to know. Mrs Farrier might gossip all she liked, but no new tales were going to begin from any careless remark of mine. I owed Mrs Ellis that much.

'There were rumours,' Ray said thoughtfully. 'When David and Angela were

71

killed, some people said it wasn't an accident.'

I stared at him, seeing Gareth's white face, hearing him cry, 'He killed my father!'

No!

'And now there's Gareth,' Ray went on, swilling the remains of his beer round the mug. 'Some peculiar things have happened to him, too. For instance, at Eastertime, when he was home on holiday, he came off a swing—a tyre swing like the ones in the garden here. He was lucky not to break his neck. The rope snapped, apparently. Then only three weeks ago there was a family party—I think it was Mrs Ellis's birthday. The lot of them went down with food poisoning. Mrs Farrier nearly walked out because of it. She thought they blamed her. But the queer thing was that Gareth was affected the worst. The rest of them were only mildly upset, in varying degrees. But Gareth was rushed into hospital.'

'Maybe he had a delicate stomach,' I said, though I felt chilled.

'Maybe so. Or maybe he's simply accident-prone ... Or maybe there's a nastier explanation.'

'Ray!' I breathed, horrified. 'Do you know you're talking slander?'

'I'm just telling you the facts.'

'The gospel according to Mrs Farrier!'

'Why should she lie? It's all true, Jane. You draw your own conclusions. Have another drink.'

'No. No, I don't think I want any more, thank you. Do you mind if we go?'

'Need some air?'

Not answering, I left my seat and pushed through the crowd to the door. The night air was cool against my face and arms but it didn't stop my brain from whirling.

'I've put it all down in a book,' Gareth had said. 'About the swing, and about the poison' ... And the pony, and the bike, my mind added. How many 'accidents' had to happen before someone did something, for Heaven's sake!

But presumably the hospital had done tests over the food poisoning, and presumably what they had found had satisfied them. And Joel had called the police about the cycle accident, and again they had been happy to conclude that it was chance. So who was I to believe a boy's wild accusations and some vicious gossip?

'It's turned cold,' Ray said from beside me, taking off his jacket. 'Here, put this round you. No, I'm okay. We'll walk briskly to keep warm.'

With his jacket and his arm around my shoulders, we walked down the lane through a dark, moonless night, with the trees sighing.

'Jane ...' Ray said as we stopped by the cottage gate. 'If there's ever anything you want to tell someone, I hope you'll feel free to come to me. A trouble shared, you know. Don't let

73

things get on top of you. The Ellises are a pretty tough proposition for one girl to handle. So if I can help...'

'Thanks, Ray,' I was grateful for his friendship. One day I might need it.

He bent to kiss me lightly. 'Don't forget. I'll be round tomorrow. See you then.'

Slinging his jacket over one shoulder, he turned away and was soon lost in the darkness. The cottage waited for me, a black shape against the shifting trees. And it was that moment that my mind chose to remember what Mrs Ellis had said about intruders at the cottage, or something which might 'disturb' me. Clamping my bottom lip with my teeth, I edged along the path, fumbling for the key.

The cottage was as I had left it. No one had been there, nor were there any strange occurrences. Though I lay awake for ages listening, there were no peculiar noises, either, only the night wind whispering in the woods.

By morning the weather had changed. The sky was heavy with cloud and a light drizzle misted along the wind as I drove to the big house. I planned to ask Gareth for details about his accident with the swing, and about the food poisoning episode, but that had to be delayed when Gareth came running down the stairs to meet me.

'*He's* in the library,' he informed me in an undertone. 'He wants to teach me equations. I'm glad you've come.'

'Your face looks a bit better,' I said.

'Yeah, it's okay. You'll tell him to go, won't you? We don't want *him* around.'

Joel was sitting at the big table, his head resting on one hand as he worked on a jumble of figures, Gareth's maths book open beside him. When I said, 'Good morning,' he looked up and for a moment searched my face as if trying to read my thoughts.

'I've been trying to remember how we tackled these things when I was at school,' he said eventually. 'He's all up the creek. This one, for instance. Look at the difference.'

Leaning on the table, I glanced at his sum and then at Gareth's. 'You're using a different method,' I told him. 'His workings are correct; he just gets the answers wrong, somehow.'

'But I don't see . . . Look, pull up a chair and show me. I'll crack this thing if it kills me.'

We spent the next half hour arguing about ways of doing equations. Joel had been at school seven years ahead of me, and in that time methods had changed, but once I had made him accept that, and shown him the new principles, he soon grasped it and almost at once saw where Gareth's problem lay.

'You obviously have a mathematical mind,' I said ruefully. 'I haven't, I'm afraid. Perhaps I should never have tried to teach him maths.'

We had both been so absorbed that we had forgotten Gareth, who had slipped away into his 'study', as they called the ante-room.

75

'I'll fetch him,' I said, and would have risen had not Joel laid his hand on my arm to prevent my leaving. It felt like a brand on my skin, the more so because I had become increasingly aware of his physical nearness as we sat together.

'Was this what you wanted to talk to me about?' he asked. 'You told Serena it was about the lessons.'

My cheeks felt hot and I hoped they were not flushed. I felt guilty, chagrined, embarrassed. 'Yes,' I lied, and pulled free of his touch. 'I . . . I think I can cope now. Thank you for your help.'

As I left my seat, Joel said, 'If I'm interfering you have only to say so.'

'You're not. No, you've been a great help. But we can't keep you from your work.'

'There's not a great deal I can do in this weather. The staff are coping with making up the orders. I was planning to pick raspberries, but if you do that in the rain they go mouldy. However . . .' he pushed back his chair and stood up, tall and athletic, regarding me with grave blue eyes, 'I'll let you get on with your own work.'

My teeth were gnawing at my bottom lip and my laugh was unsteady. 'Yes, it's time I made a start.'

'You started half an hour ago.'

'Oh, you can't count that. I was hired to teach Gareth, not you.' I felt intensely nervous, high-strung, and my voice sounded odd even to me. It was as though the air in the library was full of static, making me jumpy and ill-at-ease.

'The delay was entirely my fault,' he said.

'No! Really ... I'd never have seen the answer if you hadn't ... It's obviously just a mental block he's got. I can remove that now, I hope. It was very kind of you ...' If I had lifted my hand I could have touched him, felt the material of his shirt and the warmth of the skin beneath. That I should be aware of such things disturbed me deeply and I was unable to meet his eyes.

'Well, if you have any more problems, let me know,' he was saying.

'Thank you, I will, though I hope it won't be necessary.'

'Why?'

Startled by the question, I looked up at his face. 'Because I don't want to keep bothering you. I ought to be able to do my job without that.'

'It's not because you'd prefer to avoid me?'

'What?' I was struggling to gather my scattered wits. 'No! No, of course not. Please ... excuse me.' The library suddenly seemed vast as my shoes squeaked piercingly across the floor. It was a relief to find myself in the ante-room, where I closed the door behind me and leaned on it, turning hot and cold in turn. What on earth was wrong with me? I prayed that Joel had not been able to sense the turmoil he had caused inside me.

'Has he gone?' Gareth asked, looking up from the low round table where he was working on a model of a space shuttle. 'I'm not going back if he's there.'

'It's all right, he's gone. At least, he was going.' Thankfully, I could breathe again and my pulse was returning to normal. 'I think we can beat those equations now.'

'Oh, heck!' Gareth said feelingly.

It soon became apparent that Joel had found the key to the problem. Gareth and I worked at it for an hour, by which time his stumbling block had been erased and he was beginning to wonder why he had ever found equations difficult. Partridge brought coffee and biscuits again and we spent the rest of the morning exploring some of the vagaries of English grammar, which was my own special territory so I felt more confident.

As I went down the stairs on my way home for lunch, Irene Reid was crossing the hall.

'Mrs Ellis wants to see you,' she told me in her usual abrupt way. 'She's in the sitting room.'

'Thank you,' I said, but Irene had gone, her stiff back rapidly retreating towards the kitchen.

I found Mrs Ellis sitting by the french windows with some knitting. Outside, a patch of sunlight moved slowly across the lawns and there was blue sky between the clouds.

'It's clearing up,' Mrs Ellis remarked, following my gaze. 'Sit down, Jane. Lunch will be about half an hour. Would you like a sherry?'

'I ... didn't realise I was expected to stay again,' I said awkwardly. 'I don't want to impose.'

'You're not imposing. Pour us both a sherry. The cocktail bar is over there. I like mine dry.'

Irresolutely, I played wine waitress, though I poured only one drink. How did I explain that I was concerned that my relationship with the Ellises was becoming blurred at the edges? I was supposed to be an employee but I was being treated more like a guest. It was becoming obvious that Mrs Ellis's old friendship with my mother was more a pitfall than a blessing.

'Don't you want one?' Mrs Ellis asked as I gave her the sherry.

'No, thank you. Mrs Ellis ... I won't stay for lunch, if you don't mind. You hired me as a teacher and ...'

'Yes, I know that, my dear, but you're so good for Gareth. I want you to stay. He's more like his old self when you're around.'

'Is he?' I could not keep the amazement out of my voice.

'Yes, he is. Much more relaxed and normal.'

'But ...' I hesitated, deciding that I must clarify my position now, before the situation got out of hand. I didn't like to lie, but it seemed the only way to avoid causing offence. 'I'm afraid I've made other arrangements.'

Her disappointment was real. 'Oh, really? A date, you mean? In that case ... but in future I would like you to lunch with us. I had hoped to talk to you—about your mother and your family—but we never seem to have the chance. I'd like to get to know you, Jane.'

'That's very kind of you,' I said lamely, and turned towards the door.

'Oh, Jane ...' her voice stopped me. 'There was one thing I wanted to say. If you have problems with Gareth, bring them to me. I know Joel is officially responsible, but he's extremely busy and we want to keep as much worry as possible away from him. These domestic matters ... come and see me about them, will you?' It was said in the nicest possible way, with a smile, but all the same it was a reprimand. Serena must have told her about that episode in the greenhouse.

I was hurrying towards my car, cursing the circumstances which had brought me into all these complications, when I encountered Joel clumping along in wellington boots.

'Aren't you staying for lunch?' he asked.

'No, not today,' I said, not even pausing in my stride.

Why hadn't I listened to my intuition, which had warned me from the start that there might be hidden dangers in this seeming sinecure? Now I found myself teaching a boy who appeared to be in grave peril; a boy who himself was more of an enigma with every passing day; and besides being his teacher I was also expected to work miracles and make him 'normal'. If I ran into problems, to whom was I supposed to take them now?—To Joel at the risk of upsetting Mrs Ellis, or to Mrs Ellis, with the probability of annoying Joel? Was Gareth in danger, and if so was Joel behind all the 'accidents'? Gareth had said he was unlucky, I recalled. Maybe it was just bad luck that was dogging him.

And Joel ... I forced myself to examine my feelings for him and found they were ambivalent, to say the least. I was half afraid of him. I disliked the way he treated his nephew. But also I could not deny that I found him increasingly attractive. That was perhaps the main reason I had refused his mother's invitation to lunch again; I feared a repetition of that scrambling of my senses which had happened in the library and which I had been unable to control. It was more powerful than anything I had yet experienced, a feeling both frightening and exciting. But most of all I dreaded that he should ever suspect that he had that effect on me.

To take my mind off everything, I drove into Lincoln that afternoon, did some shopping and looked around the great Cathedral. The quietness and calm inside the Minster soothed my tortured thoughts and made my problems seem insignificant beside the nine hundred and more years of human joys and sorrows which had passed since first those elegant towers were raised against the sky. It would be all right, I thought. I had panicked, that was all, letting my imagination have its head.

I dined in town, mainly because I was too lazy to go home and cook myself a meal, though I have never enjoyed eating alone in restaurants. Another reason, which I hardly recognised at the time, was a reluctance to return too soon to the cottage. Gareth might decide to call on me, and if Gareth came would Joel be far behind?

It was after seven when eventually I drove through the golden evening light and discovered Ray Prentiss at my gate, having apparently been to call for me.

'Thought you'd deserted me,' he grinned as I climbed out of the car. 'Been shopping? Can I help?'

I let him carry my bags and packages and invited him in for coffee, declining his suggestion of a walk since I had been on my feet all afternoon, in high-heeled shoes which had made my legs ache. We sat in the front room, where I kicked off the offending shoes and tucked my feet under me, sipping the hot coffee.

'I hear Gareth came off his bike the other day,' Ray said, lounging in the opposite chair.

'His brakes were loose,' I replied.

'I heard they'd been disconnected.'

'The police said they'd worn loose!'

He raised his eyebrows at me in mild surprise. 'There's no need to go on the defensive. Nobody imagines you had anything to do with it.'

'Then who *do* they suspect?' I demanded.

'Mrs Farrier talks too much.'

'It sounds as though you've had a bad day again. Are they getting you down? I hope Joel's behaving himself. You tell me if he gives you any trouble.'

'I hardly ever see Joel.'

'I'm glad to hear it, though I wouldn't be surprised if he's only waiting his chance. No girl's safe when he's around. They fall like ripe apples from the tree.'

'Not this girl,' I said, though I was dismally aware that it was a lie. 'Anyway, Ray, are you sure you're not jealous of his success with women? Isn't it every man's dream to have an endless list of conquests?'

'Not necessarily.'

'Now who's on the defensive?' I asked with wry amusement.

From where I was sitting I could see the front hedge and part of the gateway. A movement on the road caught my attention and my heart missed a beat as I saw Joel opening the gate.

'Visitors?' Ray asked.

'It's Joel Ellis.'

83

'What did I tell you!' But to my surprise he leapt to his feet, moving so that he couldn't be seen from the path, edging towards the back door.

'Ray!' I exclaimed. 'For goodness' sake, what...'

He stopped his furtive dodging and straightened his shoulders. 'No. I have a perfect right to be here, haven't I? You invited me in. To hell with him.'

'I don't know what you're talking about,' I said, going to answer the heavy knocking on the door.

Joel stood on the path, hands thrust deep into the pockets of dark trousers. He looked tired and worried.

'Hello, Jane. Are you busy? I...' He glanced beyond me and must have seen Ray, for his mouth tightened. 'I see you are. I'm sorry.'

'Is it any business of yours?' Ray demanded belligerently, striding to my side.

'Ray!' I chided.

But his tone had raised Joel's temper. 'It might be,' he said tightly. 'Just what *are* you doing here, Prentiss? Collecting more scandal? I might have known you'd be sniffing round. Can't leave us alone, can you? Though what you hope to gain...'

Ray pushed past me onto the path, confronting Joel. 'The truth, that's all! It's time the truth was told.'

'What truth?' Joel raged. 'Damn you,

84

Prentiss, get off this property. I've told you before, you're not welcome at Huntersmere.'

'And why not? What have you got to hide?'

'Will you go, or do I have to...'

'Leave Jane alone, with you around?'

Joel stared at him as if he hadn't heard properly. 'What the hell does that mean?'

'You know what it means!'

White with anger, eyes blazing, Joel said between his teeth, 'You're clouding the issue, Prentiss. I think I told you to go. If I find you here again...'

Unable to listen to any more in silence, I burst out, 'Will one of you please explain what's going on?'

'Don't you know?' Joel snarled. 'Is he paying you for information, or are you just gossiping for the sake of it?'

Ray muttered something and the next moment his fist had shot out and Joel was sprawling backwards, falling into a rose bush, thudding awkwardly to the ground on his back. My cry of alarm echoed through the darkening woods. I found myself holding Ray's arm to prevent him from hurling himself onto Joel.

'Stop it, Ray. Stop it!'

'I'll kill him,' he said viciously, and his face was that of a stranger. 'I'll bloody kill him!'

CHAPTER FIVE

It all seemed unreal and yet it was happening—Ray in a murderous rage and Joel struggling with the clawing branches of the rose bush, his face pale with shock and a trickle of dark blood seeping from one eyebrow.

'You'd better go,' I said, and Ray stared at me open-mouthed.

'*I* had?'

'Yes! Do you want to make things worse? Please, Ray.'

'All right. But I'll be back, whatever he says. You take care of yourself.'

Numbed, I watched him walk hurriedly away and down the lane, then I bent to help Joel to his feet. The rose thorns had snagged his sweater in a dozen places and there was mud on his elbows and trousers. When he was upright he jerked away from me as if he couldn't bear me to touch him.

'Judas!' was what he called me.

I stared at him blankly, wondering what I had done, while hot tears rushed to blind me. 'Judas?' I managed. 'Why? Why, Joel?'

'You've betrayed us, that's why! What have you told him? I knew it was a mistake to have you here. I knew we'd regret it.'

'I haven't told him anything!' I cried. 'I haven't! Why should I?'

'Are you trying to tell me you didn't know he was a journalist?'

My mouth worked but no words would come. I could hardly see him any more. The daylight was waning and there among the trees it was already dusk.

'You didn't know?' Joel said in a different tone.

'A journalist ...' I breathed.

'Jane ...' His hand came against my cheek, his thumb wiping at my tears. 'Jane, I'm sorry. I thought you knew. I thought you *must* know. Please don't cry. I didn't mean ... Jane!'

The last was a whisper, his breath warm on my skin. I felt his lips on mine and suddenly his arms were round me, pulling me close to his warmth. Still crying, still dazed, I clung to him and let him comfort me with his mouth and his body hard against mine. It didn't seem strange, not on that night when everything had gone mad. I only knew I needed him and he was there.

'I must be out of my mind,' he said gruffly, holding my face pressed into the curve of his shoulder, his arms still tightly round me.

'We both must,' I muttered.

His breathless laugh sounded close to my ear. 'I don't mean this, I mean ... I should have trusted my instincts about you. I knew I could trust you, only ... I get so angry. It scares me sometimes. Everything boils up and I can't think straight ... Bless you.' He pressed a kiss

87

below my ear and stepped away from me, still holding my arms, which was just as well. If he had released me entirely I might have fallen.

I looked up at him dazedly, feeling drunk. 'Your eye ... It's bleeding.'

'Is it? It feels the size of a tennis ball.'

'You can't go home like that,' I said. 'Will you let me fix it? Come...'

The lights in the cottage helped to clear my head. He sat in the kitchen and let me bathe his face, staunching the blood. By that time there was a swelling coming over his eye. I couldn't think what had possessed Ray to hit him. It all seemed like a bad dream.

He was muddy all down his right side, where he had landed on the garden; his sweater was plucked and his hands were filthy, so that where he had touched me there were traces of mud on my dress and my face. When I had tended to his eye I went into the shower room to wash my face and hands while Joel used the kitchen sink. I was beginning to feel horribly embarrassed by the whole episode and took my time over tidying myself, noting as I brushed my hair that my eyes were still unnaturally bright.

'Do you want some coffee?' I asked as I emerged into the kitchen, but paused in concern. Joel was slumped, head in hands, at the table, and the eyes he lifted to mine were dulled with pain and weariness.

'Please. And have you got any aspirins?'

88

'Yes, of course. Headache?'

'Eyeache,' he said wrily. 'Still, I was asking for it, wasn't I?'

I dropped some soluble painkillers into a glass of water and gave them to Joel before making coffee. There was still an air of unreality about the evening, about the two of us being alone at the cottage, with Joel bruised and weary.

'You must be wondering why I came,' he said as I sat opposite to him.

'Somehow it seems irrelevant. I still can't believe all this is happening. Ray a journalist ... But what could *I* have told him?'

'I don't know,' he sighed. 'I'm paranoic about him. When David and Angela were killed—you know about that?—Prentiss was hovering like a vulture. He turned up at the house soon after my father had his stroke and I nearly belted him. I was at the end of my tether. Since then he's always been there, in the background.'

'But there's nothing he can print, is there?'

'Not yet. What he's waiting for is a big, juicy scandal that he can sell to Fleet Street and make his name. He's persistent, I'll give him that. How long have you known him?'

'I met him on Sunday morning. He was walking his dog.'

'And you were with him last night. I came to see you, fairly late. That paperwork I mentioned kept me busy until after nine. When

I saw the car was still here I wondered if you had gone to the "Bull", and there you were, deep in conversation with the enemy. Was it him you had lunch with today?'

'Today?'

'Mother said you had a date.'

'Oh—yes, I did tell her I'd made other arrangements, but . . . I'm afraid it wasn't true. I simply didn't want to stay for lunch. My position is becoming a bit obscure. I'm an employee, but your mother insists on regarding me as the daughter of her old friend and I have trouble being both.'

'But you are both.'

'Exactly. That's what makes it so hard. Anyway, I didn't see Ray at lunchtime. He was here when I got back about seven-thirty, so I asked him in and made coffee. I thought he was a friend of mine.'

'And now?'

'Now I'm not so sure. He has talked a lot about you and your family. I suppose he might have been trying to draw me out, though I promise you I haven't told him a thing. He learns quite enough from your Mrs Farrier, if you ask me. But what I can't forgive is his not telling me he was a journalist. I probably wouldn't have seen anything wrong in that if he'd been honest, but he said he worked "in an office", so he meant to mislead me.'

'I didn't break up a romantic interlude, then?' Joel said.

90

'All we've ever done is talk—and he's done most of that. He knows an awful lot about you, Joel. He told me about the Figginses, and he showed me the graves in the churchyard.'

'Did he tell you I nobbled David's plane?'

I hesitated, surprised that he should know about the rumours. 'It wasn't so much what he said as the way he put it. He was careful not to say anything that could have been construed as slander.'

'But the inference was there?'

'I'm afraid so,' I said unhappily. 'And all these mishaps with Gareth...'

'I know. I'm the prime suspect, aren't I? What really hurts me is that Gareth thinks so, too.'

I must have gasped or something, for he looked at me in surprise. 'Well, did you think I wasn't aware of it? He's told you, of course. His wicked uncle is out to murder him and grab his inheritance. Little he knows! ... It's true that David and I didn't see eye to eye. I thought he was lazy, too fond of the good life, and ... yes, if I'm honest I was a bit jealous, too. But not jealous enough to commit murder.'

He looked into his coffee ruminatively. 'My father started the market garden, you know. He hoped that David would take an interest, but he didn't. Instead he went into partnership with Alan Maine—who is now Serena's husband—but he never put much into it apart from money. Then he was killed and my father

91

taken ill, so I had to come home and take over.'

'Come home? From where?'

'Northumberland. I was a farm manager up there, for a big combine. I'd been through Agricultural College, so I was capable of running the market garden, though I was hoping my father would recover sufficiently to let me leave. It didn't happen, as you know, and anyway I'd become Gareth's guardian, so I was stuck. It wouldn't be too bad if only Gareth and I got on. Whether you believe it or not, he's extremely devious. He seems to like to goad me—as if he's trying to make me show my hand and prove that I'm the villain he thinks me. We have one battle after another—which is the reason I came out tonight for a breath of air. I thought I'd call on you to find out what you really wanted to talk about yesterday. It wasn't just equations, was it?'

'No,' I admitted. 'I've forgotten exactly what I intended to say, but I had caught Gareth out in a lie and ... It worried me. The reasons behind it, I mean. I'm sure you're right when you say he likes to goad you. I couldn't understand why he did it, though. He seems to be frightened to death of you most of the time.'

'Yes, he has played that to the hilt when you've been around. For myself it's getting so that I can't tell what's real with him and what's done for effect. I shouldn't let him get to me, but he always does ... What was it you discovered?'

'I'll show you.' Having left my seat, I hesitated, looking down at him worriedly. 'This is between the two of us. I don't want to make trouble for Gareth. You promise you won't...'

'Beat him?' Joel said with a rueful gleam in his eyes. 'It may interest you to know that I've never once hit that boy. I bluster and I threaten, but my bark is worse than my bite. I can't remember ever hitting anyone.' He lifted a hand to touch his swollen eyebrow and winced. 'Unlike some people I might mention.'

'You could sue him for assault.'

'Oh, he'd love that,' he said drily.

Going into the front room, I took the page of the letter signed 'Helena' from between two books where I had left it. I still wasn't sure that I was doing the right thing, but Joel had been frank with me and now seemed the time to have everything clear between us.

'Good Lord!' he said when he had read the page. 'Where did you get this?'

'Gareth was using it as a paper aeroplane. It was on the floor in the library when you asked him if he'd been in your room. I only found it later.'

'Oh, I knew he'd been in there. He does it to annoy me.'

'That's what worried me.'

Joel smiled at me, making my stupid heart lurch. 'Well, *don't* worry, though I appreciate your concern. It's more than I deserve after the

93

way I've behaved towards you. It's funny … I'd forgotten I'd even kept this letter. Schoolgirl stuff, isn't it? She was a girl I knew in college. Must be all of ten years ago.'

'Oh? I … thought it was recent.'

'Recent? Jane, my last girlfriend was hardly speaking to me for the past six weeks. It came to a final end on Sunday. She was furious with me for making so much of that bike incident. That's how it's been lately. There are times when I'm not fit company for another human being.'

'I had noticed,' I said with a small smile. 'But it's only when you're tired, or worried, isn't it? Your girlfriends ought to understand that. At least your mother's more observant. She told me not to bring my problems to you.'

'But you will, won't you?'

'Let's hope I don't have any more now I understand the situation better. I may be able to make Gareth see you in a different light.'

'Then you do believe me? The other day you weren't sure. That episode with the bike …' He shook his head worriedly. 'I'm still not happy about it. If you ask me, the police were a bit too ready to wash their hands of the whole thing. After all, it was only a kid on a bike and no great harm was done, but … oh, I don't know!'

'You did suggest that Gareth might have loosened the brakes himself,' I reminded him.

'The thought had crossed my mind. But if that was so he would surely have been a bit more careful. He must have come off with a hell of a crunch. Well, you've seen him. If he had known his brakes were useless, would he have ridden so fast?'

'It doesn't seem likely. On the other hand ... You remember on Saturday morning, when he came off his pony nearly under my wheels?'

His jaw tightened and his mouth grew grim, as if the memory annoyed him. 'I remember.'

'Did you actually see him fall?'

'I couldn't see clearly for the trees. Why?'

'Because ...' I nibbled at my lip uncertainly. 'I'm not sure about this, but I have the feeling that he could have stayed in the saddle if he'd tried. It was as though he deliberately jumped off and threw himself down, to frighten you.'

'Or to impress *you*.'

'Me?'

'He knew your car. It was his chance to impress on you that I was the villain of the piece. All that about my wanting him to fall ... That was for your benefit. Why do you think I was so angry? Besides ...' He bit the word off, glancing away from me.

'Besides what?'

'It sounds disloyal to say this, but ... We had planned to go riding together. We do, occasionally. As usual, we were at loggerheads, and when ...' Gritting his teeth, he went on with a rush, 'When he was mounted, he wheeled the pony into me. Knocked me flat, and rode away. Do you wonder that I was

95

chasing him?'

I could think of nothing to say. It was terrible that Gareth should so hate his uncle. But in spite of that, I recalled, Joel had been genuinely concerned when he found his nephew apparently lying insensible.

'But the bike,' he said with a shake of his head, 'is another thing altogether. That wasn't play-acting. He really was hurt. And I can't believe his brakes would have got that bad without his noticing. He's careless with the bike and doesn't clean it, but if something mechanical was wrong ... Damn it, he *knows* about those things. He'd have put it right.'

'Then you think ... you really think that someone...'

'That's what I'm trying *not* to think. Who would do such a thing? And why, for God's sake?'

Since it was a rhetorical question, I didn't attempt to answer it, though I was remembering how I had surprised Ray, early on Sunday morning, not far from the out-house where the bike was. And Ray, as I now knew, hated Joel. Would he have interfered with the bike simply to throw suspicion on Joel? With disgust I halted that line of thought. I was becoming as bad as Ray, leaping to conclusions on the slenderest of evidence. There was no point in telling Joel about it, for there was already enough antipathy between the two men.

'The trouble is,' Joel said, frowning at his clasped hands, 'that it wasn't the first accident. When Gareth was home earlier this year—it must have been the Easter holidays—he had a nasty fall from a swing. There was an old tyre hanging from an oak tree on the edge of the park. I fixed it up myself when I was Gareth's age, so the rope was pretty old. I'd been promising myself to renew it, but you know how it is. I never got round to it. So I blamed myself. The odd thing was that it didn't break at the top, where it had been rubbing on the tree; it snapped about two feet below the branch. At the time I didn't think anything of it. I cut down the rope and burned it with some other rubbish, but Gareth didn't want the swing fixed up again. When I suggested we go to buy some new rope, he gave me such a look ... I knew he thought I had caused the rope to break. That's when it all started.

'And then, only a few weeks ago, I brought him home for the weekend. We'd arranged a family party because it was mother's birthday and she likes to have a fuss made. Serena and her family were here, too. The twins were going to stay overnight, but during the afternoon Philip developed a temperature and they thought he was sickening for something, so they took him and Paula home. Mother, Gareth and I dined alone and during the night we were all taken ill—Irene and Partridge, too. They'd eaten the same meal. It was some chicken concoction that seemed to be the culprit. Most of us recovered within twenty-four hours, but mother took longer, and Gareth ... he was so ill it scared me. The doctor had him taken into hospital. He was there for about a week, and when he came out I could see that he thought *I* was responsible again. I've tried every way I can think of to prove to him that he's wrong, but he still believes it. What can I do, Jane? I'd never hurt him. How do I make him believe that?'

'I don't know,' I said helplessly.

He made a movement with his hand and for a second I thought he was going to reach out and touch me, but instead he sat back, putting more distance between us. 'I didn't expect an easy answer. But it helps just being able to talk about it to someone. I've felt so alone, besieged by the whole thing. Forgive me for burdening you with it.'

'You haven't burdened me! Most of it I knew. Oh, Joel ... It will be all right.'

'Do you think so?'

'I'm sure of it. Gareth's accident-prone, that's all. And when he realises how wrong he's been, he'll come round. He's just a mixed-up, frightened boy. He must feel alone, too. They *have been* accidents.'

'That's the only logical answer, isn't it?'

'Yes, it is.'

Joel's blue eyes searched my face soberly and rested for a moment on my mouth, making my skin prickle. 'It would be nice to believe that, wouldn't it?' he said at last, and finally the truth lay between us, bleak and frightening—we both suspected that someone was trying to harm Gareth, for reasons which we could not begin to guess at.

Sighing heavily, Joel pushed back his chair and stood up. 'It's time I was going. Mother will think I've got lost. You'll be all right, will you?'

'Why shouldn't I be?'

'I was only making sure.'

'Thank you. But it's not me who's in danger, is it? Unless there's something odd about this cottage that no one's told me. Your mother seemed a bit anxious about me, too.'

'Did she? She never wanted to put you here in the first place. But you're not afraid of being on your own at night, are you?'

'I wasn't, until everyone started asking about it. It's not ... Ray did say something about a ghost.'

His eyes flashed with anger. 'Then he should have known better! That's just a tale! But since you know about it, I expect that would be what mother meant. She's a bit gullible that way. Look, Jane, if you want to move to Huntersmere...'

'I don't. I'd only feel in the way. And Ray didn't intend to worry me. He said it was only a local legend.' Seeing the expression on his face, I added swiftly, 'I'm not defending him, Joel,
99

but you are inclined to think the worst where he's concerned. You needn't worry. I shan't repeat any of what we've said tonight.'

'If I had doubted that,' he said, 'I wouldn't have talked to you. Don't mention it at Huntersmere, either. As far as they're concerned, I wasn't here. All right?'

'Understood.'

'I'll be on my way, then.'

'Yes.'

Still he hesitated, as if he were as reluctant to leave as I was to see him go. Or perhaps he was waiting for me to see him out. But when I started to rise he said hastily, 'Don't get up. I'll ... see you tomorrow, if I can find my way home in the dark.'

'Didn't you bring the car? Oh—no, I'd have heard it.' I got to my feet, feeling that I ought to, and Joel opened the back door.

'There's a moon,' he said as he stepped into the yard.

'So there is.' Leaning against the door post, I peered up into the sky, where a few stars were sprinkled around the young moon. 'But it's not giving much light. Do you want a lift back?'

'No, thanks. The walk will do me good. Well ... good night. And thank you for the coffee—and the sympathetic ear.'

'You're welcome,' I said, a heavy sadness weighing on my spirit. 'Good night, Joel.'

'See you tomorrow.'

'Yes.'

For a few seconds more he lingered, then suddenly made up his mind and, giving me a last half-smile, was gone into the night.

I closed the door and looked at the empty kitchen, remembering Joel there. While we talked I had noticed so many small things about him which had made me feel tender—the tiny frown line between his brows; the sickle-shaped scar on his forehead, half hidden by his dark hair; the scratches on his hands from the rose thorns ... Shaking myself, I cleared away the cups and brought the others from the front room. What a crazy night it had been!

After making sure that the doors were locked securely, I took myself to bed. The bedroom mirror showed me a pale reflection as I ran my fingers over my lips, remembering Joel's kisses. To judge from what had followed, one might have thought those moments in the dusk-filled garden had never happened, for he hadn't attempted to touch me again and our conversation had been of other things. Well, what had I expected? Had I really thought that Joel cared about me? You're a fool, Janie Ashborne! He was upset, that was all. You were both upset, sent off-balance by the sudden flare of violence, and needing comfort. I told myself it had been so, but my lips still ached for the kiss he had not given me before he left, and the moon shimmered through sudden tears.

Flinging myself into bed, I lay flat on my

back, the covers pulled round my throat. Was someone trying to hurt Gareth, or were Joel and I over-reacting? And if the cottage was haunted, whose ghost lingered here? I wished I had made Joel tell me in detail. I wished I had taken up the offer of a room at Huntersmere. No, I didn't—I wished I had never even heard of Huntersmere, that I was now safely in my own bed, with my parents within calling distance.

* * *

'You look tired, Jane,' Mrs Ellis said with concern when she called me into the bright morning room the following day.

'I had rather a restless night,' I said, though even that was an understatement.

'Why?'

'Oh—you know how it is. I didn't see the ghost, if that's what you're thinking.' In the morning sunlight I could laugh at such absurdities.

Mrs Ellis, however, was concerned. 'I was hoping you wouldn't hear about that, but I suppose it was inevitable. You mustn't take any notice of it. As far as I know, it was only seen once.'

'What was it?' I asked, starting to worry in spite of myself.

'It's said to be ...' She glanced at the door to make sure it was closed. 'There was a carpenter

102

stayed in the cottage once. Actually, my husband's first wife, Elizabeth Figgins, is said to have run off with him, when she was very young. Before she married John, of course. Anyway, the affair was stopped and the carpenter went away to the war and was killed. He was seen—at least, local gossip has it that it was him—just once, in the garden, as if he had come back to look at his old home.'

And his name, I thought, was Peter. That was why the place was called Peter's cottage, though I could understand why the tale had been kept from Gareth. The Elizabeth in question had been his grandmother.

'But that wasn't what I wanted to see you about, Jane,' Mrs Ellis was saying. 'It was something much more cheerful. Your mother telephoned last night. We had a lovely chat. She sent you her love, of course, but best of all she said they would accept my invitation. They're coming over the weekend after next, on the Friday night, and I want you to come here for lunch and dinner on the Saturday, so that we can all be together. Will that suit you?'

'I shall look forward to it. Thank you.'

'As for lunching with us on weekdays . . . Joel says I'm not to insist. So please feel free to join us if you wish, though I shan't be offended if you prefer to eat elsewhere.'

So Joel had mentioned that, had he? It would probably suit him better if he did not have to face me over the lunch table every day.

He must be regretting his impulsiveness of the previous evening, so I would not embarrass him with my presence.

Murmuring something non-committal, I went on my way to the library.

That morning my pupil was nowhere to be found, neither in his study nor in his bedroom. I set out the books I intended to use and sat waiting impatiently, slowly growing more worried, until Gareth suddenly burst into the library and rushed to fling himself into his seat. His face was aglow from exertion and there was in his eyes a bright satisfaction.

'Sorry!' he gasped. 'I had something to do. Had to give a message to one of the men. What are we doing this morning?'

'I'd like you to read to me from this book.'

'History!' he groaned. 'Heck, Jane ... oh, all right. "In the middle of the Eighteenth Century, the port of London received ..."' He read on, in a dreary monotone, stumbling over a word here and there but obviously taking in very little of the sense of it. When a lawn-mower started to drone below the window it claimed his attention every few minutes and I had to keep bringing him back to the work in hand.

'Oh, stop!' I sighed eventually. 'You're not listening to what you're saying, are you? I thought you might be interested in this period. One of your ancestors made a fortune out of the tea trade, so I hear.'

104

'You mean old Josiah?' He leapt from his chair, looked out of the window, and turned to draw my attention to a portrait on the opposite wall. 'That's him, with the wig and red nose. And that's his son next to him.'

Interested, I left my seat and went to look more closely at the pictures. 'Who's the one with the whiskers?'

When there was no reply I glanced round and saw Gareth with his nose pressed against the window.

'Gareth!'

He jumped visibly. 'What? What did you say?'

'Who's the man with the side-whiskers?'

'Sir George, my great-great-grandfather. And that one over there is my grand-mother—my *real* grandmother, Elizabeth.'

Sir George had been painted in his middle age, a stern-looking man with fierce bulbous eyes. And Elizabeth—the tragic Elizabeth of the attempted elopement, the enforced marriage to a much older man, and the death at the age of twenty-two—was beautiful, fair and delicate, with a sadness in her eyes.

'You look a bit like her,' I commented, but Gareth was again staring with rapt attention out of the window.

Feeling that I had been manipulated into forgetting about lessons, I walked swiftly to join him, asking irritably if he had never seen a lawn-mower in action before.

'I'm watching what will happen,' Gareth said.

'The grass will get cut,' I retorted. 'Back to work.'

'No, please ...' He glanced at me desperately. 'Watch him, Jane.'

So I watched, and what I saw was a man riding a motorised lawn-mower in a smooth arc around the curving lawn, throwing up a spray of cuttings that fell into a neat pile to one side. There was nothing unusual in the sight, but I could feel the tension in the boy beside me.

'What are you expecting to happen?' I asked eventually, mystified.

'I don't know. But something will, you see. Joel said *I* could cut the lawn this afternoon, if it was fine, but I went and told Frank that *he'd* got to do it this morning.'

'Do you usually give the men their orders?'

He looked at me in disgust. 'I said Joel had sent me, of course. You don't get it, do you? Usually Joel doesn't let me near that mower, though he knows I can drive it. So why did he say I could this time?'

Suspecting where that train of reasoning was leading, I said worriedly, 'Gareth, you mustn't...'

'He's fixed it, don't you see?' he cried. 'He's fixed it so it will blow up or something. But I'm wise to him. It won't be me who will get hurt, it will be Frank. And then we shall *know*.'

106

CHAPTER SIX

The lawn-mower continued on its way, cutting even swathes across the big lawn.

'You're wrong, you know,' I told Gareth. 'If Joel said you could mow the lawn it was because he thought you would enjoy doing it. Now you'll miss your chance. And serve you right!'

But Gareth wasn't listening, because Joel had appeared below. Shouting, he strode determinedly towards the mower, which eventually stopped. It was evident, even from that distance, that Joel was angry. There was a brief, animated discussion and Joel turned to look at the house, making Gareth duck down to sit with a thud on the floor.

'Oh, hell!' he groaned.

'Well, what did you expect?' I asked crossly. 'And don't swear, please. Why you ever do these things...'

'Is he coming to the house?'

'Yes.' Joel was striding back across the lawn towards the steps, every line of him expressing fury. Don't be angry, I begged him silently, my forehead pressed against the glass, but I knew it was a vain hope.

Scrambling back to his seat, Gareth began to read where he had left off. '"Cotton was great, but woollens were still the greatest and by far

107

the most widely..."'

I also returned to my chair, doodling nervously on the pad in front of me, my bottom lip caught between my teeth. I wanted to see Joel, but not if he was in a temper. That morning I felt unable to withstand the blast.

The door opened and his footsteps echoed heavily across the parquet. I looked up, hoping to calm him with a meaningful glance, but his attention was fixed on Gareth, his temper under a steely control that threatened to snap at any moment. The black bruise on his eyebrow was spreading to surround the eye itself.

Pale with apprehension, Gareth watched as his uncle paused a few feet from the table.

'Since when did you take over the management of this place?' Joel asked tightly. 'I needed Frank this morning. Who gave you the right to start giving orders?'

Gareth kept his mouth clamped shut, but besides the fear there was dull defiance in his eyes.

'Answer me!' Joel roared.

'Joel...' I began in a small voice, rising to my feet.

'You stay out of this,' he ordered me, but for the first time he glanced at me and what he saw checked him, for he added brusquely, 'I'm sorry, Jane. I apologise for interrupting you again, but I want this sorted out here and now. You know what he did?'

'He told me.'

That surprised him. 'He told you? Then did he also tell you *why* he took it upon himself to rob me of an extra pair of hands, when he knows we're struggling with the raspberries?'

I couldn't answer. I couldn't hurt him by telling him Gareth's reasons, so I only looked at him unhappily.

'Didn't I tell you he goes out of his way to annoy me?' Joel asked in exasperation. 'I can't waste any more time on him now. But you can stay in this afternoon, Gareth. You can write me an essay. Jane will give you a subject.'

He turned on his heel and had started for the door when Gareth jumped up and yelled, 'And I shan't mow the lawn! Ever! You won't get rid of me that easily!'

Joel stopped, his back rigid, and when he turned his face was like stone. 'So that's it,' he said in a low voice. 'What do you think I've done to the mower, Gareth?'

'I don't know,' Gareth said sullenly, edging towards me. 'But I shan't touch it, anyway.'

'Damn it, I thought I was doing you a favour!' Joel cried. 'Jane, tell him...'

'I have done,' I said. 'He doesn't believe me.'

Joel straightened himself, eyes sparking as he stared at Gareth. 'Very well. The lawn-mower can stay where it is for now. You can keep an eye on it, Gareth. And after lunch you can watch me mow the lawn myself. When the mower doesn't run away with me, or explode, or whatever you're expecting it to do, maybe you'll have the grace to apologise.'

We watched as he left the library and I felt intensely sad for him, wishing I could go after him and offer some crumb of comfort.

'He does care about you, Gareth,' I said. 'That's why he gets so angry. He wouldn't hurt you. You must believe that. This afternoon you'll see how wrong you were.'

'I shan't,' Gareth said, plonking himself down in his chair.

'What makes you so sure?'

'Because he obviously hasn't done anything yet. He knew I'd be busy with stupid lessons this morning. I'll bet he was planning to sabotage the mower later.'

Against such stubborn hatred there was little I could say.

I did not stay at Huntersmere for lunch, but after eating a snack at the cottage climbed into the Mini and just drove, not caring where I was going. If I had stayed, I might have been drawn to watch the battle taking place on the lawn—Joel thinking he was proving something to a boy whose suspicious mind would still believe the worst.

By mid-afternoon I was in the Wolds, the pretty hills where fields of corn were ripening, where streams ran through quiet woods and villages nestled in shallow valleys. Recognising the name on a signpost, I stopped in the hamlet of Somersby and looked at the old grey

110

rectory, where the young Tennyson had lived, before going into the small church opposite to breathe the cool, dusty air and read the inscriptions. But my mind was back at Huntersmere.

As I stepped from the dimness of the church into the sunlight, I was halted by a thought that struck horror through me. Suppose something did go wrong with the lawn-mower? Joel hadn't interfered with it, but suppose someone else had—the same someone who had disconnected the brakes on Gareth's bike!

It seemed imperative that I should get back as quickly as possible, for if something happened to Joel...

Over an hour later, when I drew up outside the cottage, the extent of my helplessness hit me. I could not rush to Huntersmere to find out what had happened. They would think me interfering and probably crazy. And if there had been an accident—which I prayed there had not—they would think my concern even stranger. I was obliged to keep away, to contain my impatience until the morning, when I had a legitimate reason for going to the house, while all the time my imagination conjured up scenes of horror—the mower becoming a ball of flame; Joel injured; ambulances...

Telling myself not to be such a fool, I cooked a meal, forced myself to eat it, did the dishes and then took a shower and washed my hair. I was in my bedroom, pulling on jeans and a sweater, when I heard the gate click. Hoping that my visitor might be Joel, I rushed to the window, only to see Ray Prentiss coming up the path.

The sight of him depressed me even further, but I wrapped a towel round my damp hair and went to answer the door.

'I've come to apologise for last night,' Ray said. 'I shouldn't have lost my temper, but I thought he was going to belt me so I got in first. Is he going to sue me?'

'He said not.'

'That's a relief, anyway. I couldn't afford a court case ... Aren't you going to ask me in?'

'Should I?'

He stared at me in bewilderment. 'You're not mad at me, are you? Hell, I was defending your honour.'

'It didn't need defending, thank you,' I said crisply. 'But it isn't simply the fact that you hit Joel, though that was bad enough. Why didn't you tell me you were a journalist?'

'Because you might have suspected my motives.'

'Were they so pure, then? You tried hard enough to get me to talk.'

'Yes, I know, but ...' He sighed and pulled his mouth awry. 'Okay, I'll admit that in the beginning I did think you might be a useful source of information. That's my job, Jane—to find out the truth about things. You're closer to the Ellises than Mrs Farrier. She only gets kitchen gossip, but you ... All right, so I went about it the wrong way. I'm sorry. From here on in we won't mention the Ellises unless you want to. I promise you it wasn't only my professional curiosity that kept bringing me here. I like being with you. We can go on being friends, can't we?'

'I don't know,' I said slowly. 'It has only just occurred to me ... Mrs Farrier passes on all the gossip about Huntersmere. So presumably you knew there was a teacher coming to stay at this cottage. That very first morning, you knew who I was and why I was here.'

His expression told me that I had guessed correctly.

'What did you do, Ray?' I asked bitterly. 'Swat up some Shakespeare to impress me?'

'Oh, come on! That's hardly fair!'

'Have you been fair to me?' I demanded. 'Grief, I was really stupid, wasn't I? What a gullible little idiot you must have thought me. I listened wide-eyed to all your tales—all your despicable insinuations about Joel. You almost had me believing them.'

Ray was silent, watching me with a speculative expression. 'He's got through to you, hasn't he? I suspected as much last night. You were much too ready to leap to his defence. What was he doing calling on you at that hour, anyway? How long did he stay after I left?'

113

'That has nothing to do with you!'

'Doesn't it? Jane ... Jane, listen to me.' He caught me by the shoulders, shaking me. 'Look at me ... That's better. I care too much about you to let you do this to yourself. Don't get tangled with him. He'll use you while it suits him and then drop you like a hot brick. You don't want to be just another name on a long list, do you? I know he's attractive. He has some mysterious ... charisma, I suppose you'd call it—something that draws women like bees to the honey. But for your own sake you must resist it. You'll only get hurt.'

'I'm not that stupid,' I said flatly.

'Nobody's saying you're stupid—you're just vulnerable. I cursed myself all the way home last night. I really handed him an ace, didn't I? I bet you had him in and patched him up ... Well, of course you did. And then what happened? He exerted his magic charm and wrapped you round his finger. I should never have left you ... He did stay, didn't he?'

'Yes,' I said reluctantly, shrugging free of his grasp.

'And?'

'And nothing! We talked, that's all. You've no right to question me about it, Ray. If I get hurt—and I'm not saying I will—it's my own business. Please go away and ... I'm sorry, but perhaps it will be best if you don't come back. We shall only quarrel.'

He stepped away from me, frowning. 'It's

your own choice. If you'd rather be made a fool of by a good-looking liar than be friendly with an ordinary bloke who just happens to have principles ... Good luck to you. When he lets you down, don't come running to me for comfort.'

As he turned away I closed the door, feeling both angry and apprehensive. How dare he twist things so that I felt guilty when it was he who had been in the wrong? Oh, but suppose he was right about Joel?

I closed my eyes, torn between tears and fury, and in the darkness behind my eyelids logic came to my rescue. Ray couldn't be more wrong. Apart from that brief, unreal few minutes when he had held me in his arms, Joel had never made any attempt to charm me. Rather the reverse. He had displayed the full biting force of his temper and told me of his problems in all their worrying detail, and what I had seen had been a man, not a seductive Casanova—a man with faults as well as virtues; a man who had worries, who could be tired and feel pain; a human being beset by problems, facing them alone, needing someone to turn to. That was what had attracted me, not his dark good looks or his blue eyes, and certainly not his smooth line in chat.

Or was that exactly the trap that Ray was afraid I might fall into?

And was Joel even now lying hurt, or worse?

Furious with myself for the inner conflict in

115

which I was caught, I towelled my hair vigorously and curled up in a chair to read.

I was still worried the next morning when I drove to Huntersmere, but it was a relief to see that all the lawns had been cut. Someone had raked up the cuttings and taken them away, so the park looked neat again.

I saw no one at the house until I found Gareth sitting in his place at the library table. As I went in, he slapped shut the book he had been reading—the novel I had bought him.

'Good book that.'

'I'm glad you like it. How are you this morning?'

'Okay. I scratched the scab off my knee last night. There was blood all over the bed.'

'Oh, Gareth!' I sighed. 'Why are you such a pickle? But everything's ... everything's all right, is it? Nothing happened?'

'How do you mean?'

'The lawn-mower...'

'Oh, that! I told you nothing would happen.'

My legs went weak with relief and I flopped down into my chair, while Gareth watched my face with interest.

'I thought you didn't believe that he...'

'I don't! It's wicked of you to suspect such things.'

'Then why do you look so relieved?'

'Because for all I know, *you* might have fixed that lawn-mower just to get back at Joel—as you did when you flung yourself off your pony in front of my car.'

Gareth coloured up to his eyes. 'I was only trying to get you on my side.'

'I *am* on your side, and so is Joel.'

'Then why did he disconnect my bike brakes?'

'He didn't!'

'And why did he cut the rope on my swing? I could have been killed. They all said so. But he burned the rope so nobody could find out. *And* he tried to poison me!'

'Gareth! Listen ... hasn't it occurred to you that all these things might be accidents? And if they are, don't you realise how much you're hurting Joel by constantly suspecting him? How would you feel if someone you loved thought that ...'

'He doesn't love me. He doesn't even like me. Nobody does. Even my Mum and Dad sent me to boarding school because I was a nuisance.'

'*I* like you,' I told him. 'That's why it worries me that you think such terrible things. I can ruin you, poison you with hate, and it's all so unnecessary.'

A spark of malicious amusement lit his eyes. 'Did you see his face yesterday? He's got a real black eye. Walked into a door.'

'And that pleases you? That isn't very nice.'

He blinked at me in puzzlement. 'Do you like him?'

'Yes, I do. I only wish the two of you could

117

be friends.'

At that moment, Joel came in, looking relaxed and almost happy. He strolled unhurriedly across the library, wearing a shirt that was the same azure blue as his eyes, and actually smiled at me—which sent me into confusion.

'Good morning. Am I interrupting again?'

'We hadn't really started,' I said, self-consciously tidying books, trying to look efficient.

Joel perched on the corner of the table. 'Good. I came to warn you that there might be some noise on the back stairs. The builders have arrived.'

'Builders?' I queried.

'We're having trouble with dry rot. They're going to take the whole staircase out and put a new one in, so you may find it a bit distracting. If it gets too bad, you can move to the study downstairs.'

Leaving his seat, Gareth padded to the opposite wall and opened a door I had never noticed before because it was cunningly disguised to look like a continuation of the book-shelves, complete with false books.

'Be careful, Gareth!' Joel called, adding to me, 'I'm not sure exactly how bad it is, so we haven't used those stairs since the trouble was discovered. How are you, Jane? You look a bit pale.'

Under the scrutiny of those blue eyes, my

face must have lost its pallor. 'I'm very well, thank you. How's your eye?'

'It feels better than it looks. I walked into a door, you know.'

'So I heard.'

'I thought you might.' A wry smile crossed his face as he glanced to where Gareth stood in the doorway looking down at the workmen below, whose voices echoed hollowly up the stair-well. 'The lawn-mower,' Joel said in an undertone, 'worked fine.'

'I heard that, too,' I replied in an equally quiet voice. 'Thank God for that. Didn't you stop to consider that whoever ... did those other things, if anybody did ...'

'Of course I considered it. That's why I had to do it myself. If the thing *had* gone up, with me aboard, it would have proved I wasn't responsible.'

I stared at him, admiring his courage and yet horrified by the risk he had taken. 'Are you mad? Didn't you check first?'

'And have Gareth think I was repairing it? No. Anyway, nothing untoward occurred. Maybe there is no bogey man. Have you ... seen the door again?'

'Which door?'

'The one who gave me this black eye.'

'Oh ... yes, he was round last night. I didn't tell him anything.'

'What *did* you say?'

I was saved from having to reply by the

return of Gareth. He closed the door in the far wall and it became again part of the book-case.

'How long are they going to be?' he asked.

'Weeks, if they run true to form,' Joel replied with irony. 'By the way, Gareth, it's your birthday on Monday, isn't it?'

'So what?' Gareth said rudely.

'I've been wondering if you would like to go to the pictures as a birthday treat. On Sunday evening, maybe. They're showing that film that you've been on about.'

'"Galaxy Four Thousand"?' Gareth said eagerly, though his enthusiasm was tempered by his very real distrust. 'I dunno. Who would I go with?'

'Me—and Jane, if she'll come. No doubt you'll feel safer with her around.'

Gareth gave him a bitter glance and said again, 'I dunno.'

'Well, think about it.'

'I'd like to see that film,' the boy admitted grudgingly. 'It's a super film, Jane. There's this alien monster, all slime and six eyes, and space pirates ... Will you come?'

There was nothing I would have enjoyed more than spending an evening with Joel, but that was just asking for trouble. I looked up at him, saying slowly, 'It's very nice of you, but I'm sure there must be someone else you'd rather take.'

'One of my many girl-friends, you mean?' he said levelly.

'Well, yes.'

'Perhaps you would rather go alone with Gareth.'

'I thought you wanted to give him a birthday treat?'

'I did, but since neither of you seem eager for my company...'

'Oh, heck!' Gareth broke in. 'We'll end up not going at all, at this rate. Can't we all go? You will, won't you, Jane? You said you liked him.'

I glared at him furiously, making him squirm. 'Well, you did. So what's the hassle? Why does there have to be a big argument about everything?'

'I'm beginning to wish I'd never suggested it,' Joel said. 'It's only a trip to the cinema, not a week in a nudist colony!'

'Joel!' I gasped, but all he did was widen his eyes at me, while Gareth giggled—though that in itself was a minor miracle. The tension between them had evaporated and for a while this was a normal family occasion.

'All right, I'll go,' I conceded.

'Great!' Gareth jumped up in excitement. 'I'll go and get the paper and see what time it starts.'

He ran from the library more animated than I had ever seen him, and as I watched him Joel touched my arm with one finger. Startled, I looked up at him.

'Thank you, Jane. If I'm ever going to get

close to Gareth, I shall need your help. He trusts you. If he sees that you and I are friends, maybe ... well, there's a chance. It's been ages since I was able to make him laugh, so that's a beginning.'

'I'm glad,' I said, though my thoughts were bleak and I was remembering what Ray had said—'He'll use you while it suits him and then drop you like a hot brick.' That was all I was to Joel—a useful bridge to Gareth.

'You were going to tell me what happened between you and Ray Prentiss,' Joel reminded me.

It was my wounded feelings that made me reply, 'No, Joel, I wasn't. I don't happen to think it's any of your business,' and I made myself busy opening books, sorting out the ones I wanted to use next, doing anything that would avoid the necessity of meeting his eyes.

He slipped off the table and came to stand at the window, behind my left shoulder. 'The grass looks better, anyway,' he said irrelevantly. 'Have you seen the cathedral? It looks magnificent at night, when its floodlit. It seems to hang in the air ... If you've made other plans for Sunday you should have said.'

'What?' Realising that he thought I had made a date with Ray, I turned and saw him in profile, his hands deep in his pockets. The blue shirt was patched at the elbow and his hair needed trimming, making me feel suddenly tender towards him.

122

'I haven't made other plans,' I said quietly. 'I told Ray I didn't want to see him again.'

He took a deep breath and let it out slowly, still staring at the view outside. 'You didn't have to do that.'

'I know. But that's the way it happened.'

The air between us had become electric again and this time I was sure that he was as aware of it as I was. But the moment passed because Gareth came bouncing in with the local evening paper and we turned our minds to planning the outing to the cinema.

*   *   *

When Friday dawned—the end of my first full week at Delton—I was starting to think that I might enjoy the summer after all. I seemed to be making progress with Gareth; I was settled at the cottage (apart from a few lingering doubts about the ghost); Gareth and Joel appeared to be making headway in their relationship; there had been no more 'accidents'; and, yes, I was falling in love with Joel, foolish though it might be. I seemed destined to fall for men who were out of reach, or unsuitable, but the end of the summer, when I would have to leave Huntersmere, was a long way away and I decided not to think about it.

The morning started quietly enough, apart from the growing noise of demolition from the back stairs. We were doing some French

123

translation when a movement caught my eye and I saw the far door opening slowly, as if of its own accord. A small blonde head peeped round, and Philip, Serena's little boy, marched on sturdy legs to stand in the centre of the library with his arms folded in a most officious attitude which made me wonder which grown-up he had seen in that stance.

'Gaweff!' he said shrilly. 'You dot to tum!'

Gareth looked up, glowering. 'What for?'

'My mummy said so.'

'That's Philip,' Gareth informed me. 'My cousin. He's got a twin sister called Paula.'

'Twickly!' the little boy ordered impatiently. 'Gaweff!'

'I'm busy,' said Gareth. 'Go away, Philip.'

A look of fury contorted Philip's face as he ran back to the door. 'I'll tell my mummy of you,' he threatened as he left.

'Perhaps your aunt wants you for something important,' I said.

'Well, she needn't have sent that little twit to give me orders. I can't stand either of them. Paula's wet. You've only got to touch her and she cries.'

'But they aren't very old, don't forget.'

A few minutes later, Serena appeared, dressed in lime green with her hair caught up at the back of her head.

'Goodness, what a hive of industry,' she remarked with a laugh. 'Hello, Jane. Hello, Gareth. I know you're awfully busy and you

124

just love doing lessons, but can you tear yourself away long enough to come and look at your birthday present?'

'Birthday present?' Gareth showed a little more interest. 'Where?'

'Downstairs. It's too big to bring up. I know we're three days early, but we're off on holiday tomorrow and I'm dying to watch you unwrap it. Come on. Alan's downstairs. You come, too, Jane. This might be worth watching.'

Gareth ran ahead of us and as we went down the stairs he dashed into the sitting room, saying, 'Hallo, Alan. Where is it?'

'Diplomatic little devil, isn't he?' Serena said with a twinkle.

Her husband was a big, easy-going man with fair hair that he was rapidly losing, and an incipient paunch. When we were introduced he said with a grin that there hadn't been any teachers like me at the schools he went to.

The present, it seemed, was outside, so we all moved onto the terrace for the ceremonial unveiling. Alan Maine brought a chair for Mrs Ellis and she was enthroned with the doll-like Paula on her knee, while Serena stood near holding Philip by the hand. On the drive stood the Maines' blue estate car, with a small horse-box behind it.

'Another pony?' Gareth said, trying not to sound disappointed.

'Come and see,' Alan invited, starting down the steps.

125

Serena caught my eye and gave me a conspiratorial wink. 'My dear brother is going to have a fit, I'm afraid.'

The back of the horse-box was opened and Gareth stood transfixed for a moment before rushing up the sloping rear-board and out of sight, with cries of, 'Oh, gosh!' and 'Wow!' and similar exclamations of wordless delight.

'I knew he'd be pleased,' Serena said. 'That's what birthdays are for.'

But I saw Mrs Ellis give her a worried glance and when I saw what they were bringing out of the horse-box I knew why. The present was a small motor-cycle, the type my brother Ray would have called a mo-ped.

Gareth was leaping up and down in uncontrollable excitement as Alan held the bike. He was urging Gareth to sit on it, to try it, and Gareth didn't need telling twice. He flung his leg over the seat and crouched at the handlebars while Alan showed him the switches.

'Not that he needs telling,' Serena said. 'Don't look so worried, mother. He's had several rides on one at the stables.'

As was inevitable, the moment came when the engine was turned on, its buzzing sounding loud in the silence, and the bike roared away down the drive, despite the fact that Gareth had no protection, no helmet, only his jeans and T-shirt. I was dismayed by the irresponsible attitude of Serena and her husband, who only stood and cheered the boy on.

I sensed, rather than saw, Joel's arrival. He stood at the end of the terrace, having come up the ramp, evidently growing more angry with every second; then suddenly he started forward, towards the steps.

'Oh, Joel, don't!' Serena cried. 'He's having such fun.'

'Fun?' He whipped round to stare at her, his lips white with rage. '*Fun*? Don't you realise he might kill himself? Those things aren't toys!'

Gareth had driven up onto the lawn and was going round and round, describing curving figures, oblivious to everything but the joy of riding.

Again Joel started forward, only to be stopped by Alan.

'Come on, man. Didn't you ever have a motor-bike? What's best—for him to have one now and learn to ride it properly, or to go straight onto the road at sixteen?'

'Blast you, Alan!' Joel raged. 'I told him he couldn't have a motor-bike. Why the hell didn't you tell me...'

He ran down the steps two at a time, skirted the blue car and raced, gesticulating, out to the centre of the lawn where Gareth was doing a figure of eight.

'Why did Joel have to turn up and ruin it?' Serena said. 'He and David used to ride motor-bikes when they were Gareth's age. He's just

127

being unreasonable.'

The roar of the bike, as the throttle was opened fully, drew our attention back to the lawn. Gareth had seen Joel coming and was rapidly moving away from him. Joel halted, his arms falling to his sides as he realised he couldn't possibly chase the machine. Taking a wide U-turn round an oak tree, Gareth headed back, going up through the gears until he was at full speed, heading straight for Joel. He was crouched low, staring at his uncle, and Joel stood as if frozen.

I heard Mrs Ellis gasp. My own heart was thudding in alarm. Then at the last moment it was Joel who moved, flinging himself aside to land headlong on the grass while the bike roared on, across the drive onto the far lawn, turning in a broad loop.

'He must have got the wheel in a rut, or something,' Serena said breathlessly. 'Why on earth didn't Joel move sooner? He must have scared Gareth silly.'

'They were testing each other's nerve,' was Alan's opinion as, laughing, he watched Gareth bring the bike to a halt at the foot of the steps. 'Well, Gareth? Good?'

'Super!' His face was scarlet. 'I ... I couldn't seem to turn the wheel. I didn't mean to hit him.'

'Of course you didn't,' Serena soothed. 'We all know that. It was his own fault for standing in the way.'

By that time, Joel had picked himself up and was striding towards us, brushing bits of grass from his clothes, his face like a storm-cloud. Without a word he ran up the steps, brushed between Serena and me, and went into the house.

I wanted to go after him, but of course I couldn't. I could only stand with the others, doing my bit towards the awkward silence, and I hated Serena and Alan for their blindness. Hadn't they seen the menace in Gareth as he drove directly at Joel? Were they so complacent that they couldn't see the harm they had done?

The tension broke. The twins began to run about the terrace; Serena helped her mother to her feet; Alan was ruffling Gareth's hair, telling him he was going to be a great driver.

It was only then that it occurred to me that there was someone else who might benefit from Gareth's death. If Gareth could not inherit, presumably David's estate would be divided between his half-brother and -sister, Joel and Serena. Serena, whose husband had 'lost the main source of his capital' when David died. And it was Alan and Serena who had bought Gareth the potentially lethal motor-bike.

CHAPTER SEVEN

'Whatever happened to Joel's eye?' Serena asked as she helped her mother into the house.

'He says he bumped into the edge of his door,' Mrs Ellis replied.

'A likely tale! It looks more as though one of his girlfriends turned nasty. Oh, Jane ... don't bother with the chair. Alan will bring it in. You know, I don't think Gareth is going to be able to concentrate on lessons this morning.'

I followed them into the hall, saying, 'I thought the same myself. I'll just go and pack the books away. We may as well call it a day until Monday.'

In the library, I put the books into neat piles as I always did at the end of every session. I could hear the motor-bike running on the drive and when I glanced out of the window Alan was riding the machine while the twins and Gareth sat on the steps. The builders were busy behind the hidden door, but I was more aware of the door to the ante-room, standing open in the corner. Was Joel in his room? What was he thinking?

Knowing that I should leave, I stood for a while biting my lip in indecision, then went softly into the toy-filled 'study' and knocked on Joel's door.

There was no reply.

'Joel?' I said in a low voice.

He might have gone straight through the house and back to the greenhouses, I thought. Then as I turned away he said from inside the room, 'Come in, Jane.'

Opening the door slowly, I saw him lying prone on the bed, his face turned away from me and covered by one arm.

'Are you all right?' I asked.

'Yes. Come in and shut the door.'

I closed the door and stood by it, feeling terribly uncertain for there was no way of telling what mood he was in.

'Are you packing up?' he asked.

'Yes, I ... I thought I might go home for the week-end. It's not all that far, and I could be back in time for the pictures on Sunday—if you still intend to go.'

His hand clenched and unclenched, gathering handsful of the coverlet. 'Do you think I was unreasonable?'

'About the motor-bike? No. I'd have been furious myself. They ought to have asked you first. And they should have bought him a crash-helmet. I can't understand their attitude.'

He rolled over onto his back, an arm across his eyes. 'They believe that children should be allowed to do more or less as they please. That's why the twins are turning into such little horrors. But Gareth's *my* responsibility, not theirs. If something happens to him...'

'If something did happen ...' I said awkwardly, 'would Serena and Alan benefit?'

'What?' He sat up, showing me his ravaged face and tousled hair. 'Oh, I see what you're thinking, but ... no, that's not the answer.'

Throwing his legs over the side of the bed, he rubbed his face, leaned his head in his hands. 'No, they're just trying to please Gareth. It's me who's the spectre at the feast, as usual, another reason for Gareth to hate me. You should have seen his face. He'd have killed me if I hadn't moved. He really hates me that much.' After a moment he turned his head to look at me. 'I notice you don't deny it.'

'He must have lost his head. He did say he couldn't turn the wheel. Alan thought he was testing your nerve.'

'Alan would! The man's a fool. What shall I do, Jane? I can't very well forbid him to ride his own motor-bike.'

'You could insist he wears a crash-helmet, and leathers. My brother always did. And you could teach him to drive it properly. You're right, it's not a toy—it's a dangerous weapon ... You weren't hurt, were you?'

'Shook myself a bit. Nothing serious.' He gave an unhumorous laugh and looked at his spread hands. They were trembling. 'I was so mad I thought I was going to explode. I felt so bloody impotent!'

'I know,' I said.

Without looking at me, he held out his hand.

'Come here. Please.'

I moved slowly and stood before him, watching his bent head, while he took both my hands in his. Now I was trembling, too, wanting so much to take him in my arms and comfort him. Then he reached out and pulled me to him, his face pressed to my waist, his arms like steel bands around me, and I let my fingers stroke his hair, tidying it. I understood that he needed someone to lean on and I was fiercely glad that I was there.

'Don't go home,' he muttered in a choked voice. 'Please don't go home. I can't ...' He stopped abruptly and tore away from me, wrenching himself to his feet, going to stare out of the window with one hand clawing through his hair. 'I'm sorry. Of course you must go home if you want to. Your parents will be glad to see you. Don't tell them too much, though,' with another attempt at a laugh, 'or they might not let you come back to this mad-house. Gareth would be sorry about that. He's grown very fond of you. He doesn't take to many people. You must be very special. Look ...' He swung round to face me, throwing out a hand in appeal. 'Forgive me for all this. I'm making a damn fool of myself. None of this is your problem. You go home and have a good weekend. Forget about Huntersmere. I feel terrible about involving you. I should never have talked so much the other night. It's my problem and mine alone. Why I ever ...' He

133

broke off, glancing at the door, where his sister was coming in.

She seemed surprised to find me there. 'Hello? What's happening? Are you going to sulk up here all day, Joel?'

'I must go,' I said, edging past her. 'Excuse me.'

I left, because I had no right to be there, because the curiosity in Serena's eyes was unbearable, and because Joel had made it plain that I was to stay out of it. He was right, it wasn't my problem—but it felt as though it was.

Once I returned to the cottage, I discovered all manner of reasons why I could not possibly go to Sheffield for the week-end: there was washing, cleaning and shopping to do; I didn't feel like driving all that way; if I went I would only blurt out the whole story to my parents. All these excuses I found to reinforce my real reason—Joel had asked me not to go.

Having done my washing, I left it to drip in the yard, using a line and some pegs which I found in the shed. There was a good breeze and the sun was warm, so the clothes should dry. I spent the rest of the afternoon on hands and knees with a brush and pan, which was exhausting, but all the time I was hoping that Joel might come. He didn't, and I was annoyed with myself for expecting him.

However, as I took the dry clothes from the line that evening I did have a visitor—Gareth, on his new motor-bike. I heard the engine putter to a stop and a few moments later when Gareth came into the yard I was relieved to see him wearing a white crash-helmet and a black leather jacket, plus a big grin.

'Hell's Angels have a new recruit,' he announced, turning round to display the jacket.

'So I see. Where did you get that outfit?'

'In town. Joel took me this afternoon. He's being pretty decent about it, really. I've got my own garage, so nobody else can touch the bike. That was *his* idea.'

'It's more than you deserve!'

He pulled a face, but he had the grace to look ashamed. 'Aw, heck! I didn't mean anything. I wasn't going to run into him. I'd have swerved if he hadn't moved. I thought he was going to say I couldn't keep the bike.'

'And for that you'd have injured him, maybe maimed him for life?'

Gareth considered me with puzzlement. 'Why are you angry?'

'Because you're an ungrateful little beast! Oh ... I've been worried sick, that's all, here on my own not knowing what was happening. You wouldn't understand. So ... you're happy now, are you?'

'Sure. The bike's great! Just what I wanted. And *I'll* have the keys to my garage, so nobody can mess about with it. You haven't really seen it, have you? Come and have a look.'

We admired the mo-ped and Gareth showed me all its features. He even said I could have a ride on the pillion, if I wanted—an offer I declined.

'Well, I'd better go,' he said at length, itching to be back aboard the machine. 'I just thought you'd like to see my outfit. And don't worry, Jane. I'll be careful.'

He shot off down the lane back to Huntersmere, as confident as if he had been handling the machine all his life. I was glad that Joel had decided to compromise, but I wondered how he really felt about giving Gareth his own garage.

On Saturday morning I had a letter from Mum which was full of questions and excited references to their planned week-end with Muriel. She also said, 'I'm glad to hear you're making friends over there and hope you'll introduce us when we come', which puzzled me, for Mrs Ellis would perform what introductions were necessary.

Later, I went to the village shop for a few necessities. The woman who served me must have been Ray Prentiss's mother, but if she knew who I was she gave no sign of it.

As I was leaving the shop, a car squealed to a halt across the road and when I looked round, wondering who could be in such a hurry, Joel was leaping from the black saloon, impatiently waiting for a van to pass. If I hadn't known better, I might have thought he was delighted to see me.

'Jane!' he called as he strode towards me. 'I thought you'd gone home. Let me give you a lift.'

Without pausing, he relieved me of my shopping basket and took my elbow, hustling me back across the road to his mother's car.

'Why did you stay?' he asked.

'I had a lot to do.'

'Oh? Such as what?'

'Housework. Shopping. You know.'

He started the car, giving me a smile. 'No, I don't know. I thought you were miles away. I nearly phoned Sheffield last night to see if you'd got home safely. Good job I didn't. Your parents would have been worried.'

'But Gareth knew I was still here. He called last night.'

'He didn't tell me.' Again he shot me a smile, seeming in high spirits.

'What happened to your own car?' I asked.

'Nothing. I've just been to fill this one up. I'm taking mother and Gareth to see some friends after lunch. Damn nuisance. If it wasn't for that I could have taken you out—shown you the countryside.'

'I've seen the countryside. Well, some of it.'

He drew up outside the cottage and turned to face me, his arm along the back of the bench seat. 'You mean you don't want to go out with me?'

'I mean I'm quite capable of entertaining

myself!' I retorted sharply, mainly because I couldn't let him see how I really felt. 'I knew I would have the week-ends on my own. It doesn't worry me.'

Considering me thoughtfully, he said, 'You're here as a teacher, and nothing else?'

'That was the arrangement. You said it yourself.'

'A week ago.'

'Does one week make any difference?'

'You ought to know the answer to that.'

I tore my gaze from his and looked round the car. 'I won't keep you. Where did you put my basket?'

'It's here.' He reached to the back seat, gave me the basket with my few items of shopping and sat watching silently as I fumbled with the unfamiliar door handle. At last it came free and I stepped out hurriedly.

'Thank you for the lift. Have a good day.'

'And you,' he said, but his eyes reproached me, asking questions, and I ran away from him only to find myself in tears as I reached the door of the cottage.

It was a lonely, miserable day, the cloudy sky only adding to my depression. I was puzzled by my own emotions, which were in turmoil, but that was entirely my own fault. Hadn't I been warned, by both Ray and Serena, not to let myself get involved with Joel? Yet that was exactly what had happened, and every time I saw him it grew worse. It was something more than the friendships I had formed in college and the silly infatuation with Doctor Anthony Burns. This time every aspect of my being was drawn to man—physically, emotionally, and mentally. Sometimes he made me feel weak and helpless, but at other times I was fiercely protective of him, ready to fight his enemies, wanting to share his problems. But I kept remembering Serena's jibe about 'another notch on Joel's hunting knife', and I was terribly afraid that, to him, that was all I would be—just a summer dalliance, which was bound to end when the new school year began.

There was a good play on the radio that evening, which briefly took my mind off my problems and kept me so enthralled that I didn't bother to put the lights on and draw the curtains but let the dusk fill the room with misty shadows. I was listening with my eyes closed, better to imagine the scene, when a sound outside made me glance at the window. A male figure stood among the rose-bushes, a shadowy mass in the twilight.

A male figure ... the carpenter went away to the war and was killed ... seen in the garden, as if he had come back to look at his old home ...

I sat petrified, my hand to my mouth, and saw the figure move. He came slowly to the window, made a shield with his hands, peered in ...

Yelping with fright, I leapt out of my seat. The shadowy figure backed hastily away.

139

'I'm sorry!' his voice came faintly through the glass. 'I thought you were out. Sorry.' And he retreated. A few minutes later I heard a car start up in the lane.

I swiftly drew the curtains, switched on the lights, locked the doors. Even if he wasn't a ghost, what had he been doing? It wasn't Joel, or Ray. My memory flitted crazily ... intruder ... bike ... swing ... Probably no connection at all, but I was covered in goosepimples and my heart was beating double time. By the time I calmed down again I had missed the end of the play.

*　　*　　*

The black car from Huntersmere passed again on its way to and from morning service at the church, but I didn't see who was in it. During the afternoon, Gareth called in to make sure I remembered to be ready at six o'clock for the cinema trip, and although I despised myself I became more excited as the day passed.

By ten to six I was ready, wearing my prettiest dress and high-heeled sandals, my hair washed and brushed till it shone, perfume dabbed in appropriate places. I kept asking myself why I was making all that effort, but was pleased I had when Joel arrived in a smart suit. Gareth was more casual in jeans and a bomber jacket, sitting in the back of his grandmother's car as I took the front seat.

'Ready?' was all Joel said, regarding me as if he thought I might bite.

Nearly all the way into Lincoln, Gareth told us about clips from 'Galaxy 4000' which he had seen on television, and when we joined the short queue outside the cinema he pointed out the pictures in the display, telling us who the characters were.

'It sounds as though you've already seen most of it,' Joel commented as we moved towards the cash desk. 'You two get some sweets while I get the tickets.'

The cinema was half empty, glowing with dim orange lights. Gareth dived straight for the front row of the circle and I ended up sitting between him and Joel, when I had planned to make sure that Gareth sat in the middle.

Inevitably, the show began with advertisements, followed by a feature on sky-diving. Then the lights went up for the interval and Gareth clambered past us to rush for an ice-cream.

'He's got more energy than I have,' Joel said. 'You're very quiet. Enjoying yourself?'

'Yes, thank you. Are you?'

'I might prefer the back row.'

Surprised, I looked fully at him for the first time.

'Though not with Gareth along,' he added. 'Have I told you you look marvellous?'

'No.'

'You look marvellous.'

141

'Thank you.' Flustered, I glanced up the steps to see how long the ice-cream queue had grown.

'You're quite safe,' Joel said drily. 'Gareth won't be long.'

'It's not that,' I denied. 'I wanted to tell you ... There was a man in the cottage garden last night. I hadn't put the lights on, so he thought I was out. When he saw me, he apologised and rushed away.'

'What time was this?'

'Around half past nine, I think.'

'Maybe it was the ghost.'

'If I had known you would make a joke of it,' I said tartly, 'I wouldn't have told you!'

'Well, what ... oh, hello, Gareth. Got what you wanted?'

Gareth had treated us each to a tub of ice-cream, which we ate as the big picture started. The movie was a spectacular space epic, full of amazing special effects.

Some time later, Joel casually laid his arm along the back of my seat and leaned across to murmur, 'Were you frightened?'

'By what?' I hissed, keeping my eyes on the screen.

'The man in the garden.'

'Yes, a bit.'

He was very close to me in the gloom, his breath warm on my cheek. 'You smell marvellous, too,' he whispered.

'Watch the film!' My nerves were jolting

madly, making me breathless.

Joel fell silent, but his arm remained in contact with my shoulder blades and I knew that he had his eyes on me as often as on the screen. Whenever I try to recall the story of that film, all I remember is sitting next to Joel, my whole being alive with excitement because of his nearness. I kept reminding myself about notches on knives and names on a long list, but it made no difference.

It was Gareth who again monopolised the conversation on the way home. He leaned on the back of the seat between us, recalling details of scenes in the film which I could hardly remember, but I was pleased that he had enjoyed the evening. For once he was just an ordinary boy, full of youthful enthusiasm.

At last the car pulled up outside the cottage and Joel switched off the engine.

'You wait here,' he told Gareth. 'I'm just going to make sure there's no one hanging about, and see Jane safely inside. I won't be long.'

As we crossed the road, Gareth rolled down the car window and called after us, 'Give her a kiss from me!'

'Cheeky brat!' Joel said under his breath, leading the way down the path and round to the back door. 'Got the key? Thank you.'

He switched on the kitchen light. 'Everything okay here. I'll just check the rest.'

'There's really no need ...' I began, but he

143

was gone to look in the front room and climb the stairs.

'Nobody here,' he informed me when he returned. 'You see, I didn't think it was a joke. I don't like the idea of your being here alone if there are strange men lurking.'

'There was only one,' I objected. 'And he wasn't exactly lurking. Anyway, wasn't it your idea to put me in this cottage?'

'Still holding that against me, are you? I've told you, if you want to move to the house...'

'I don't.'

'No,' he said, and his eyes were bleak. 'That would mean seeing me too often ... What have I done, Jane?'

'You haven't done anything! Whatever makes you think...'

'I can sense it. Something happened on Friday. Since then you've been ... unapproachable. If it wasn't something I did, then what is it?'

'I really don't know what you're talking about,' I said, turning away to fill the kettle to give me something to do, because what I wanted to do was to be in his arms.

'Jane, please!' He was beside me, wresting the kettle from my grasp. Between us we dropped the thing and it clattered to the floor, soaking my dress on the way, a pool of water spreading on the mat.

'Now look what you've done!' I cried, unexpected tears jerking into my eyes. 'Why don't you leave me alone!'

He grabbed the nearest cloth to hand, which happened to be a towel, and went down on his knees to mop the floor.

'Leave it!' I exclaimed. 'I'll do it. Just ... go away, Joel. Go away!'

For a moment he froze where he was, his head bent, then stood up brushing his hands, pulling his jacket straight. When he looked at me I was stricken by the hurt in his eyes, but before I could do or say anything the door burst open and Gareth came in.

'I can't stay out there on my own!' he complained. 'It's scarey. The trees are whispering. I kept thinking I saw somebody in the woods.'

'I was just coming,' Joel said, laying a hand on the boy's shoulder. 'Come on, Gareth. It's way past your bedtime.'

'I can lie-in in the morning. It's my birthday. We shan't do school-work, shall we, Jane?'

I shook my head, swallowing the knot of tears in my throat. 'No. Have a day off.'

'Is something wrong?' he asked. 'Why are you crying?'

'I'm not! Good night, Gareth. Have a happy birthday.'

Uncertainly, he looked from my face to Joel's. 'You'll be coming to my party, won't you? Granny Muriel said I could invite you.'

'She'll come,' Joel said, propelling his nephew out of the door. 'Let's go.'

I was alone, the kettle at my feet, my dress sticking coldly to my legs, the towel a soggy mess. As I bent to pick it up my tears burst like a dam and I wept helplessly, leaning against the kitchen cupboards. How had it all happened? It had promised to be such a happy evening, yet somehow it had turned into a disaster.

By the time I went to bed, after mopping the floor and hanging the mat out to dry, I felt as limp and wrung-out as the towel. Memories haunted me all night—being close to Joel in the cinema; his face, like a wounded deer. I hugged my pillow, soaking it with stupid tears.

I was woken by the sound of Gareth's motor-bike buzzing up to my gate. Reaching for my watch, I was dismayed to see that it was ten o'clock, and as I threw back the covers Gareth started hammering on the back door, shouting, 'Jane! Jane!'

When I opened the door, my dressing gown clutched round me, I was met by a pale, sullen face with red-rimmed eyes.

'I'm not going back!' he announced, marching in to thump down in a chair.

'Oh, Gareth!' I sighed. 'What's happened now?'

'I'm sick of them, that's what! I hate them both!'

A weary depression assailed me. 'Both of whom? And where's your crash-helmet?'

'At home.'

'But you promised Joel...'

146

'I don't care! I thought he was starting to like me, but he was rotten this morning. Rotten! He never even wished me a happy birthday. Oh, I wish I was dead!' He slumped across the table, his head on his arms, sobbing violently.

Worriedly, not knowing how best to deal with the situation, I touched his shoulder and was astonished when he flung his arms round me and hugged me, much as Joel had done three days before. But this time I was not obliged to cover my feelings. I knelt beside him, holding him tightly while he wept on my shoulder. The tough motor-bike rider was only a motherless boy, after all.

'Please don't cry,' I begged him. 'Please, Gareth.'

After a while his sobs diminished and he wiped his eyes on my dressing gown, still resting against me, his fingers clawing at my back in silent agony.

'I told her to go to hell,' he said miserably.

'Who?'

'Granny Muriel. I broke a cup and she got mad, so I told her to go to hell. She cried.'

'I'm not surprised,' I said, my own voice husky. 'Look ... come into the bathroom and let's clean you up, then you can tell me the whole story. Come on. We'll get all this sorted out between us.'

He stood docilely and let me wash his face, his eyes filled with misery. I used a towel gently, mopping up the trickle of tears that still fell, and on impulse kissed his shining cheek. My reward was a quick hug and an arm about my waist as we returned to the kitchen.

A glass of milk and a bowl of cornflakes—he had not had any breakfast—dried the last of his tears and made him able to talk.

'I woke up early. I was excited about my birthday. I put my radio on and I was singing. Then Joel came banging on the door, yelling at me to shut up. He called me a ... an inconsiderate little nuisance. So I turned the radio down. I was ever so quiet. I was, Jane! But he kept slamming around in a temper. I think he stubbed his toe. But when I went to see if he was okay he told me to mind my own business and I said I was glad he'd hurt himself and ...' He heaved an expressive sigh. 'You know how we get. He told me to stay in my room. He said I wouldn't get any presents if I didn't behave, so ...' another sigh, 'I chucked some things round my room and waited for him to come, only he didn't. It was Irene who came. She got angry and went to tell Granny Muriel, so when I went down for breakfast *she* was mad at me. I didn't mean to break the cup. I just put it down a bit hard and it broke and there was coffee all over everywhere and she shouted for Irene and I said she wasn't my real grandmother, and ... oh, everything went wrong, Jane.'

'Yes, it sounds like it.' I touched his hair in understanding. 'We used to have family rows,

148

too. It's natural. What happened then?'

'They told me to tidy my room, only I didn't. I sat around thinking what I could do to pay them back, and then I thought I'd run away.' His eyes filled with tears again. 'Only I didn't have anywhere to go, except here.'

Touched, I put my arm about him. 'I'm glad you came. It's nothing so really awful, you know. Tomorrow you'll laugh about it. But you see ... when people live together, they're bound to have disagreements now and then, even though they love each other. You and Joel are too much alike. You've both got awful tempers and you say things you don't mean. He's probably feeling as wretched as you are.'

'I'll bet he's not,' he said moodily. 'And I'm not like him. I'm like my real grandmother Elizabeth. Irene says so.'

'Whatever Irene says, you're also like Joel. That's not so strange. Your grandfather was his father. And he's very concerned about you—worried that he might not be doing the right things for you. He's trying to take your father's place, but he has no experience of being a father. Do you understand that?'

Gareth nodded, though I doubted whether he did understand, not fully.

'Would you like me to come back with you?' I asked. 'The sooner you tell them you're sorry, the sooner it will be over. Your grandmother ... She is your real grandmother, Gareth. She brought your father up and she loves you. Just because she isn't related by blood doesn't mean she doesn't care about you, or that you shouldn't care about her.' I was putting it badly, I thought, and perhaps it was too adult a concept for him to grasp anyway.

He agreed to return to Huntersmere, as long as I went with him to act as mediator. Wondering what the outcome would be, I went upstairs to get dressed and was just fastening the belt on my jeans when the unmistakable sound of Joel's sports car came down the road and stopped. At the same moment Gareth scrambled up the stairs in a panic.

'It's Joel!' he gasped.

'I know. You stay here. I'll talk to him.'

Joel must have sat in his car for several seconds, probably trying to cool his temper, for when I opened the front door he was climbing from the vehicle. Trying to ignore my own personal feelings, I went to meet him and we stood with the gate between us, myself ready for anything and he looking coldly angry.

'I thought he would be here,' he said, glancing at the motor-bike. 'He runs to you like a homing pigeon. I suppose you know what happened?'

'Yes. And he's going through hell because of it.'

'Mother isn't exactly leaping around with joy,' Joel said grimly. 'She's worked herself into such a state that Irene had to send for me.

The whole household's in a spin because of that selfish little ... Send him out here. He can come home and apologise.'

'We were just about to do that,' I said. 'Joel ... he's really feeling wretched. It's a pity this had to happen, today of all days.'

There was deep bitterness in his eyes. 'The whole thing's my fault, of course. I got out of bed the wrong side. I ought to have held my tongue and let him have things his own way— because it's his birthday.'

'I didn't say that.'

'No, but you meant it. All right, you take him back. He'll be happier that way.' He turned away, making for the off-side of his car, saying over his shoulder, 'And tell him not to worry about my laying any more clouds over his birthday. I'll keep away. You'll both enjoy the party better if I'm not there.'

'Oh, Joel!' I exclaimed, torn between anger and sympathy. 'You're behaving like a child yourself. Of course he will want you to be there. You're part of his family. Don't ruin all the progress you've made these last few days.'

He looked at me across the roof of his car, his mouth twisting. 'You've made the difference in him, not me. He's made it abundantly clear how he feels about me. And so have you. I'll leave you to enjoy each other's company while you can, without my snarling things up.' Jerking open the car door, he threw himself into the driving seat.

151

'Well, all right!' I said loudly. 'Go off and wallow in self-pity, if you want! I'm sick of being your go-between, anyway!'

As I ran back to the cottage, the car roared away, sounding as furious as its driver must have been.

'Gosh!' Gareth said. 'You really told him ... What's the matter?'

'Nothing!' I snapped, fighting back tears. 'I just wish I'd never come here, that's all. All the huge egos battering at each other, and I'm in the middle ... Oh, listen to me. Now *I'm* feeling sorry for myself.'

Gareth was looking at me with a hurt expression that reminded me sharply of the way Joel had looked the previous night. 'Do you really wish you hadn't come?'

'What? Oh—no, of course I don't.' I gathered him to me and kissed his forehead. 'I'm upset. I hate quarrelling with Joel. He said he's going to stay away all day.'

'Good!' said Gareth. 'He can stay away for ever, for all I care.'

The tragedy was that at that moment he meant it.

We eventually walked to Huntersmere pushing the motor-bike because I refused to let Gareth ride it without his helmet. The machine was put into one of the stables and safely locked away before we went to the house.

Mrs Ellis was arranging flowers in the sitting room and I was depressed when she greeted us with a long face—the face of stern authority demanding penance.

'Well, Gareth?' she said expectantly.

He hesitated, glanced up at me, then stepped forward saying, 'I'm sorry. I didn't mean to be rude. I'm sorry.'

'Very well,' was the cool reply. 'We'll say no more about it if you go to your room straight away and clear up the mess you made. Then I may decide that you deserve to have presents at tea-time. And while you're about it, make your peace with Joel. He's in his room getting changed.'

Gloomily, scuffing his feet, Gareth left the room.

'I'm sorry you had to become involved in this,' Mrs Ellis said to me, reaching for the walking stick she had hooked over the table. With its aid she moved slowly to an armchair. 'I dislike these kinds of upsets. This one has given me a migraine. If you had heard him ... you would have thought he hated me. Of course, Joel isn't blameless. I'm aware the day started badly for both of them, but even so ... However, I'm sorry Gareth saw fit to bother you. I must confess that when you came here I never imagined he would take to you so quickly. He seems to have formed a very strong attachment to you.'

'The attachment is mutual,' I said. 'I'm very fond of him.'

'Yes, so it would appear.' She gave me a

153

hard, searching look. 'Perhaps I'm getting old. I'm afraid I find very little about him that is lovable. He's noisy, and disobedient. You saw, of course, that he tried to run Joel down with that terrible machine last Friday? Serena and Alan made light of it, I know, but it sent shivers up my spine. Why does he hate Joel so much?'

Didn't she know? I wondered. Had Joel never told her that his nephew suspected him of several murder attempts? How on earth had he kept it from her?

'It's almost as if someone had poisoned his mind,' she went on. 'I've even begun to wonder if I should consult a specialist about him, but that seems such a drastic step. I was terribly worried ... This motor-bike. It was unforgivable of Serena and Alan to buy such a thing without consulting us first, though I think Serena managed to talk Joel round. I really thought things were improving. Then last night something happened again. Did Gareth misbehave while you were out? Joel was in a terrible mood when he came home, but he wouldn't tell me why.'

I opened my mouth to defend Gareth but stopped as I realised who had been the cause of Joel's 'terrible mood'. It hadn't been Gareth.

'I only hope nothing of the kind occurs while your parents are here,' Mrs Ellis was saying. 'I should be so ...' She stopped in surprise, glancing at the door where the butler had appeared. 'Yes, Partridge?'

The old man seemed agitated. 'I'm sorry to disturb you, madam, but it's master Gareth. He seems to have fallen down the back stairs.'

CHAPTER EIGHT

I ran down the hall in panic, to where Mrs Farrier stood in an open doorway wringing her hands and saying, 'Oh, my Lord! Oh, my Lord!' Beyond her, Joel knelt over Gareth's still form among the debris left by the builders—plaster and bits of rotten wood. The bottom half of the stairs was missing.

Pushing past the distraught cook, I stepped into the stairwell so that I could see Gareth's white face, a trickle of blood mingling with the dust in his hair.

'He's not ...' I began, and stopped because I couldn't say the word.

Joel glanced up at me, his own face pale with shock. 'He's alive, but I daren't move him.'

'Have you sent for an ambulance?'

'Partridge has.' He twisted to look over his shoulder at Mrs Farrier. 'For God's sake, don't stand there snivelling! Go and make some coffee, or something.'

Wiping her eyes on her apron, Mrs Farrier departed, but her place was taken by Irene, who asked what had happened.

'I don't know,' Joel said distractedly. 'I was

in my room. I thought I heard that top door slam, but there was no one in the library. When I looked down here I saw him like this. God knows I've told him often enough to keep away from these stairs, especially since the builders started.'

'Why aren't they here today?' I asked.

'Some trouble with their transport, so they said.'

'You think he fell?' Irene said gruffly.

'I don't know what ...' He saw the look on her face and his mouth went grim. 'Go to hell, Irene!'

Before she turned away she gave me a significant look which said that she knew what had happened, all right. Gareth and Joel had been at loggerheads, hadn't they? Both of them upstairs. Arguing again ... She thought Joel had thrown his nephew down the stairs. As I watched her walk into the kitchen I felt sick.

By that time Mrs Ellis had managed to walk down the hall with the help of two sticks. She stood a few feet from the door, her eyes wide with fright. 'How bad is he?'

'Bad enough,' Joel said tersely. 'Concussion, and I can't tell what other damage. At least he seems to be breathing easily, and his pulse is reasonably strong. Mother ... you can't do any good standing there. Go and watch for the ambulance. You go with her, Jane. There's nothing anyone can do until they come.'

I spent the next half hour wandering from

156

the sitting room where Mrs Ellis sat by the window to the stair-well where Joel knelt anxiously by the crumpled boy, constantly bending to listen to his breathing and check his pulse. At last the ambulance came tearing down the drive and the men hurriedly brought out a stretcher.

'I'll follow them,' Joel said as Gareth was carried from the house. 'Mother, phone Trimble and tell him I can't keep that appointment, will you? I'll phone you as soon as there's any news. And Jane ...' He laid his hand on my arm absent-mindedly, 'will you stay with mother?'

'Yes, of course,' I said.

Lunchtime came and went without news. Mrs Ellis and I sat in the dining room, but neither of us ate much and neither of us mentioned the other 'accidents'. Afterwards we waited in the sitting room and when, eventually, the phone rang, I leapt to my feet.

'Yes, answer it, Jane,' Mrs Ellis said, seeing my hesitation.

Rushing to the shrilling phone, I lifted it to my ear. 'Yes?'

'Is that you, Jane?' said Joel's voice. 'Thank heaven for that. He's going to be all right. He's conscious and able to talk. He dislocated his shoulder, but there are no bones broken. They'll keep him in for a few days because of the concussion, but it looks as though he was lucky. He must have bounced.'

'Thank God!' I sat down in the nearest chair, shaking with relief, and relayed the good news to Mrs Ellis, who burst into tears.

'Are you still there?' Joel asked in my ear.

'We're both of us crying with relief. We've been so worried.'

'So have I, but ... That's not all. I shan't be home yet. I have to go to the police station.'

'The ... where? Why?'

'Gareth told the doctor that I pushed him downstairs,' he said. 'They sent for the police. I'm going to have to do a lot of talking. And don't be surprised if the police turn up there. You'd better prepare mother. I really don't know what time I shall be home—if at all. Can you handle things that end?'

'Yes!' I said breathlessly, stunned. 'Yes, of course. I'll stay with your mother. Joel, they surely don't believe...'

'I don't know what they believe. It's going to be up to me to convince them. Janie ... I'm sorry if I'm using you as a go-between again, but I don't know who else to ask.'

'I'm only too glad to be here,' I said. 'Don't worry about anything. Just ... come home soon.'

'I will, if I can. Thanks, love. 'Bye.'

'Jane!' Mrs Ellis gasped as I put down the receiver. 'What is it? What did he say?'

I crossed the room slowly and sat down on the settee near to her chair, feeling numb and appalled by what I had to do. 'Mrs Ellis ...

158

apparently Gareth has accused Joel of pushing him down the stairs.'

'What?' One ringed hand went to her throat. 'No! Why would he ...? The fall must have damaged his brain. Joel would never hurt Gareth.'

'I know that. But the doctor was alarmed enough to call the police. Joel has to answer some questions. It's just routine,' I added swiftly, because she looked as though she might pass out. 'Obviously they will have to look into it, but since Joel is innocent he will soon be home. Please don't worry, though ... he did say the police might come here.'

'What for?'

'Presumably to look at the stairs and ask questions. Don't look so alarmed. They'll soon find out that Gareth is mistaken.'

'Yes, but ... Jane, why should Gareth tell such an awful lie? What has Joel ever done to him? That wicked, wicked boy!'

'He's not wicked, he's frightened! He has been in the wars lately, hasn't he? He fell off the swing; he was ill with food-poisoning; he came off his bike. And now...'

'But they were accidents. Accidents!'

'Gareth doesn't think so, and neither does Joel. And I'm afraid that Gareth thinks Joel has been responsible for what's happened.'

She stared at me for long, silent moments, then croaked, 'Did Gareth tell you all of this?'

'Some of it. The rest I heard from Joel.'

'You mean, he knows? Then why hasn't he told me? I knew there was something behind Gareth's attitude. And Joel ... this is what has been worrying him. This is why he's been so irritable lately. But who could have put such wicked ideas into Gareth's head? ... Joel hasn't been arrested, has he?'

'No, I don't think so. They would need more evidence than just Gareth's word, surely? And they won't find any evidence because Joel hasn't done anything.'

She thought about that for a while and then relaxed with a sigh. 'You're right. Of course you're right. The whole thing is foolishness, dreamed up in that child's imagination. He's never been the same since David and Angela were killed. That's what it's all about, isn't it? He's still ... unsettled. Yes, that's it. My dear ... would you be so kind as to go and tell the kitchen the news about Gareth? They'll be as anxious as we were. And while you're there, tell them we'll have some tea now. I could do with a cup.'

By 'the kitchen' I assumed she meant her three employees, whom I found busy at various tasks—Mrs Farrier was preparing vegetables while Partridge cleaned silver, and in a corner of the kitchen Irene Reid sat poring over a list. They all expressed delight and relief to hear that Gareth was not seriously injured, but I sensed the uncertainty in them about the cause of his fall.

'He was very lucky,' Mrs Farrier said.

'Somebody was,' Irene added, and the butler and the cook glanced worriedly at her and then at me, as if to see whether I understood the inference. It was obvious that they had all three been speculating and I knew that Ray Prentiss would soon have some more ammunition for his anti-Joel campaign.

'Gareth *fell* down those stairs,' I said.

'Nobody said he didn't,' Irene replied.

'Nobody needed to say it.'

They looked at one another meaningfully, and Partridge shook his grey head. 'I always did say Sir George should never have made Miss Elizabeth marry the Brigadier,' he said irrelevantly. 'That's when the rot set in. That's what killed Miss Elizabeth. Died of a broken heart, she did. The Ellises never did belong here. It's a Figgins house.'

'Upstarts, that's what they are,' Irene said. 'Sir George would turn in his grave to see what goes on. You don't know the half of it, Miss Ashborne.'

'It's not like it was in the old days,' Partridge agreed with a sigh.

'But these aren't the old days!' I exclaimed. 'If that's the way you feel, why don't you leave?'

'Well, don't look at me, dear!' Mrs Farrier blustered. 'I just do a fair day's work for a fair day's pay. It's none of my business who does what. But these two have been here a long time.

161

It's their home.'

'Nowhere else to go,' Partridge said, breathing on a spoon before buffing it again.

'And Miss Reid's been here since she was four years old,' Mrs Farrier told me. 'Isn't that right, Miss Reid?'

'Quite right, Mrs Farrier. Elizabeth Figgins was my cousin—ah yes, Miss Ashborne. That's one of the many things you don't know. When my parents died Sir George brought me here to be a companion to poor Elizabeth. I've been here ever since.' She stood up, supporting her paralysed arm with her other hand. 'Thank you for bringing us the news. If there's nothing else...'

Aware that I was being dismissed, I said shortly, 'There is. Mrs Ellis would like some tea, please.'

'For two?' Irene enquired.

'Yes, please. Thank you.' I left with as much dignity as I could summon and behind me I heard Mrs Farrier say, 'Getting a bit big for her boots, isn't she? Who does she think she is?'

It annoyed me that for a few minutes I had forgotten that I, too, was an employee at Huntersmere. That day I had been treated like a good friend by the family, but that hardly gave me the right to criticise the staff.

We were drinking tea when the police arrived in the shape of a fat detective sergeant and the young constable who had been to Huntersmere the previous week to investigate

162

the trouble with Gareth's bike. The constable was sent to talk to the staff while the sergeant spoke with Mrs Ellis and myself, asking what we remembered of that morning's occurrences. He already knew that there had been quarrels in the house.

Eventually he asked to be shown the scene of the accident and Mrs Ellis asked me to perform this chore. I showed the sergeant the bottom of the back staircase and then led him up the main stairs to the library, though when I went to open the disguised door he prevented me, saying something about fingerprints.

Next he wanted to see Gareth's room, and we both saw the mess that the boy's temper had made. It looked as though a whirlwind had hit the room. Stepping over the strewn bricks and books, the sergeant opened the middle drawer of the tallboy and rummaged under the sweaters there, bringing out an old school exercise book which he flipped through with interest. A shiver ran through me as I remembered Gareth saying, 'I've written it all down, in a book, so if something else happens they'll know he did it.'

'You're his teacher then?' the sergeant asked me over his shoulder. 'What sort of boy would you say he was?'

'Intelligent. High-strung. A bit mixed-up—because of his parents' death, I think.'

'Truthful?'

'Not entirely. He ... has this thing about his

163

uncle. He veers between fear and defiance. They do quarrel, but ... Joel would never hurt him.'

He looked at me enquiringly, one eyebrow raised. 'Whose side are you on—the boy's, or the uncle's?'

'Both! I believe someone is trying to hurt Gareth and I understand why he suspects Joel, but he's wrong. There must be someone else.'

'Who, for instance?'

'Well, *I* don't know!' I said helplessly. 'That's for you to find out. But there have been too many accidents for them all to be accidents.'

'I'm inclined to agree. The boy is very definite that someone did push him down those stairs. He said at first that it was his uncle, but later he admitted that he didn't see who it was. He came up here to clear up this mess and see his uncle, but he wasn't too keen on another confrontation so he thought he'd take a look at what the builders were up to. Putting off the evil moment, so to speak. And someone pushed him. That's what he says. His uncle was up here at the time, I gather.'

'So I understand. He was changing out of his working clothes. He had an appointment with someone.'

There were more questions, some of them seeming irrelevant. I couldn't tell what he was thinking, but when he left he took with him the exercise book which I had no doubt contained

164

a full account of Gareth's version of the affair.

I didn't tell Mrs Ellis about the book—she was worried enough as it was, seeming drained by the day's upheavals and the after-effects of her migraine. We dined together and sat watching the shadows lengthen across the park.

'If Joel doesn't come back ...' she began.

'He will! You know what the police are like. They'll want to be thorough. And then they'll let him come home.' I was almost pleading with her to believe it, for my own fears were growing.

'But he's been gone for so long, Jane. If only Serena hadn't gone on holiday ... I don't even know exactly where she is. Some caravan park in Devon. I don't think I could bear to be alone tonight. I don't like to ask you, but ...'

'I'll stay, if it's necessary. But there's time yet.'

The sun went down in clouds of gold and dusk veiled the park, deepening into night. Just when I was thinking that I must go back to the cottage and pack an overnight case, lights turned in through the gate and swung around the drive, accompanied by the coughing roar that could only be Joel's car. I ran to the window, watching as he parked by the steps.

When he came in he looked dreadfully tired. His hair was dishevelled, his tie loose and his collar undone, but he was home!

'Joel!' Mrs Ellis reached out towards him.

165

'Oh, my dear!'

He came and took her hands, bending to kiss her raised cheek. 'Hello, mother. I'm sorry if you've been worried, but we had to go over everything in detail and then they kept me waiting for ages while they typed my statement.' Straightening, he turned to send me a tired smile. 'Thanks for staying, Jane. Come and sit down and I'll tell you both about it.'

'Do you want anything to eat?' Mrs Ellis asked.

'No, thanks. I'm past being hungry. What I need is a good stiff drink.'

'We all do. Jane, dear, would you mind?'

I was only too pleased to do anything for Joel, so I poured him a scotch and soda, gin and tonic for his mother and helped myself to a sherry, while Joel began to recount the story of his absence. He had told the police everything he knew, everything he suspected, and when they had brought the exercise book with Gareth's account in it he had been obliged to go over the whole thing again, point by point.

'But at least there's one good thing come of it,' he concluded. 'It's made them begin to look seriously into the affair.'

'But Joel ...' his mother said worriedly. 'There's nothing to look into. It has been a series of freak accidents. You can't really think that ... It's too awful. It can't be true!'

'Let's hope that's what the police say,' Joel

replied, rubbing his face and yawning. 'God, I'm exhausted. I'll just take Jane home and...'

'No, you won't,' I interrupted. 'I'm perfectly able to walk.'

'And you're far too tired, Joel,' his mother added.

'I'm not letting her walk back to that cottage at this time of night,' he said stubbornly, heaving himself upright. 'Come on, Jane, I ... Whoa!' Swaying dizzily, he sat down again. 'Hell, what did you put in that whisky?'

'Just whisky,' I said. 'You're out on your feet. So I'll go. Good night, Mrs Ellis.'

'Janie ...' Joel called as I made for the door, and when I looked round he threw me something that turned out to be a set of keys. 'Use my car. Please. I'll worry myself sick if you try walking through those woods in the dark. I'll come for the car tomorrow.'

'I'm honoured,' I said. 'Thank you. Good night.'

I had only ever driven Mum's Mini, but after a little fumbling I got the sports car started in the right gear and headed it slowly for home, enjoying the fact that it was Joel's and he had preferred to trust me with his car rather than have me walk home alone. It had been a terrible day for everyone—especially Gareth, whose birthday had been a disaster from beginning to end.

Since Joel had said he would come for his car, I did not go to Huntersmere the following

167

morning. With Gareth in hospital there would be no lessons, so I had no real reason to go to the house, though I waited in growing impatience until a policeman arrived to take a set of my fingerprints 'for elimination'; then I knew what was keeping Joel.

The policeman seemed to know very little and said even less, departing as soon as he had what he came for.

Wishing that I knew what was happening at the house, I made myself some lunch, more for something to do than because I was hungry. I was washing up when the knock came on the back door.

'Did you think I'd been arrested?' Joel asked with grim humour, seeing my relief. 'No, not yet. You wouldn't believe it, but I've been trying to get here all day. I thought I'd do some work first, then the police were crawling all over the place, then Frank had a crisis he couldn't cope with, and then mother sent for me, insisting that I ate lunch.' He spread his hands expressively. 'Now I have to go and visit my loving nephew. Heaven only knows when I'll have a minute to myself. I don't suppose you'd care to come along? Gareth might like to see you even if he refuses to see me.' Although the words were light they were underlaid with pain.

'I hope one day he realises what he's doing to you,' I said. 'Just let me get my jacket—and Gareth's birthday present.'

168

The day was overcast but there seemed no threat of rain. Soon we were heading away from Delton, along the winding lanes.

'I hope I didn't damage the car,' I said.

'Not that I can tell. Anyway, she's had a few knocks in her time.'

'Gareth said you'd only had it a month. I expected a new one.'

'Good Lord, if you think I could afford a new one of these you've got the wrong idea about the state of my bank balance.' He flung me an amused glance. 'Jane ... I haven't thanked you for yesterday.'

'I don't need thanking. I was pleased to help.'

'That isn't what I meant. I haven't thanked you for believing in me. You were the only one who didn't instantly find me guilty—apart from mother, who didn't understand the implications anyway. At least, if she did she preferred to stick her head in the sand and pretend it would all go away. She was doing the same this morning—telling the police there were natural explanations for everything.'

'There still might be,' I said, though I didn't believe it. 'I mean ... there was no one in the house yesterday except the people who are always there.'

'As far as we know,' Joel qualified. 'Someone might have got in without being seen. I've been through every other possibility and nothing fits. You and mother were

169

together, so that eliminates the two of you. Mrs Farrier ... well, she's a gossip, but she's a good worker and I can't imagine what motive she might have. Irene and Partridge always have regarded mother, Serena and me as interlopers, but they're all for the Figginses and Gareth is the only one left of that blood. Which leaves me—and I know I didn't do it. So we come to a blank wall. A mysterious Mister X.'

He was right. There was no explanation.

Gareth was in a large medical ward, halfway down the room among men with varying ailments. Most of the patients already had visitors and as we approached Gareth's bed we saw that someone had forestalled us. I felt Joel tense as he recognised Ray Prentiss and I myself felt a rush of anger. Was he trying to get information from Gareth?

'I, er ... just called in to see how he was,' Ray said, prepared to bluff it out.

I ignored him, because Gareth was more important. He looked wan and sorry for himself, one of his arms supported by a sling, and when his eyes flicked to Joel they filled with fear. I sat down on the bed beside him, saying, 'Hello, Gareth,' and to my surprise he flung himself into my arms, holding me tightly, his face buried in my shoulder.

Behind me, Joel said grimly, 'Get lost, Prentiss!'

'I wouldn't sully myself in your company,'

Ray muttered. 'Filthy lecher! You don't know a decent girl when you see one.'

By the time I had twisted round to look at him, mystified by the irrelevant insult, he was striding away with Joel staring after him looking evil.

'Don't let him be angry with me,' Gareth begged in a choked whisper. 'I really thought it was him.'

'I know,' I breathed back. 'But you were wrong. You didn't say anything to that man, did you?'

He shook his head, his fingers digging into my arm, and I realised he was afraid to face Joel. He was using me as a shield, but I couldn't extricate myself without using force. I sat there holding him, stroking his hair, closing my eyes against the tears which threatened.

'I knew *you'd* be welcome,' Joel said, a hint of bitterness in his tone. He felt excluded, of course.

I reached behind me, found his jacket, pulled until he moved to where I could see him. 'He expects you to be angry. You're not, are you?'

'I was, but ... in his shoes I'd probably have thought the same.'

Gratefully, I touched his hand and he caught my fingers in his, so that I was captured by both uncle and nephew. 'Did you hear that?' I asked Gareth. 'It's all right, darling. Joel understands. You were hurt and you were afraid, but you're safe now. We both love you

171

very much.'

'That's right,' Joel said. 'Have they said when you can come home?'

'No, not yet,' Gareth mumbled.

Joel looked helplessly at me, and suddenly remembered the package he was holding. 'Hey, look, Gareth. Jane's brought you a birthday present. You missed all that. We'll have to have the party when you come home.'

Slowly, Gareth drew away from me, rubbed his pyjama sleeve across his eyes and chanced a glance at the gaily-wrapped parcel. 'What is it?'

'Open it and see,' I suggested.

He did so, awkwardly because one hand was painful to use, and revealed the box with the picture of what the kit inside would make—a model of the pirates' space ship from 'Galaxy 4000'. The sight brought a smile to his face.

'Thanks, Jane. It's great. I needed something to do. It's so boring in here.'

Joel's fingers gave mine a painful squeeze before he released me. The worst was over. I really believed the wounds would heal, though it would not happen overnight.

When we left the hospital, Joel was very quiet, but I thought little of it for he hadn't said much all the time we had been with Gareth. But when the silence continued even after we left the worst of the Lincoln traffic, it became worrying.

'Are you all right?' I asked.

'Yes. Why?'

172

'You're unusually quiet. Gareth will come round, you know. I'm sure of it.'

He made no reply and I saw him watching the road, seeming withdrawn.

'Joel, what is it?'

'Nothing!'

'There's no need to snap my head off.'

He glanced at me with cold eyes, saying brusquely, 'I'm sorry.'

'So you should be! Honestly, you and Gareth are so alike it's incredible. I'm beginning to understand his moods, but you're a mystery. I thought you'd be pleased at having made a start at being friends with him again ... It's not something I've done, is it?'

'Oh, no!' His tone was so sarcastic it had to mean the opposite.

'Joel ...' I said wearily. 'Don't make me start playing guessing games. What have I done wrong?'

'Nothing. You've been just perfect, wonderful, marvellous. I'm extremely grateful. Ignore me. I'm just being childish.'

Sighing, I turned to look out of the side window away from him. 'The corn's ripening well, isn't it?'

'Blast the corn!' Joel said viciously, and slammed the brakes on so hard that if we hadn't been wearing seat-belts we would both have gone through the windscreen. Before I had recovered my breath, he said flatly, 'I'm jealous.'

173

I stared at him, wondering if I had heard correctly. 'Jealous? Of what?'

His hands were so tightly clasped on the wheel that the bones showed white through his skin. He restarted the car, throwing it into gear, making it surge forward.

'You can't say something like that and then just leave it,' I protested, and was flung to my left as we hurtled round a corner. 'Joel! Are you trying to kill us both?'

He eased his foot off the accelerator so that we slowed to thirty miles an hour, which was still quite fast for those twisting, narrow lanes, while I searched my brain for an explanation.

'Oh, Joel … Gareth will be the same with you if you give him time. It's just that he responds to affection. My family are very demonstrative, so I'm used to touching people I care about, and that's what Gareth needs. And it's easier for a woman, anyway. I didn't mean to come between you. I was only trying to…'

'Shut up!' he snapped.

Hurt and offended, I settled back in my seat and didn't speak or look his way again. Even when we stopped at the cottage I undid my seat-belt in silence, my mouth clamped shut, and climbed from the car with my face averted. He made no attempt to stop me but drove off in a cloud of fumes, the engine snarling.

That, I decided, was the end. I had tried to help and all I had done was cause more trouble.

174

Now Joel was angry because I had managed to do what he had failed to accomplish—to come close to Gareth, win his confidence and his affection. Yet wasn't that exactly what Mrs Ellis had asked me to do?

I thought it all out while I had a meal and then I began to pack. It would be at least a few days before Gareth came home and even then he would not be fit enough for lessons, so there was no point in my staying. Tomorrow I would go to see Mrs Ellis and explain that to her, suggesting that when she felt Gareth was fully well again she could consider whether she wished to send for me.

My leaving needn't prevent my parents from coming for the eagerly-anticipated weekend. I could tell them I was coming home until Gareth was well and let the full truth wait until later—if I ever felt able to tell the full truth. Perhaps I would never be able to share the secret of my feelings for Joel.

I sat down on the bed beside my half-packed case, my head heavy with unshed tears. Outside the Mini was already loaded with most of my belongings, only a few things left to pack in the morning. When I left, it would be for good. I was sure of that.

Something I remembered made me smile bitterly to myself. Joel had said that sometimes he wasn't fit company for another human being and I had replied, 'It's only when you're tired, or worried. Your girl-friends ought to

175

understand that.' How unbearably smug of me! Now I knew that I didn't understand him, either.

But despite everything I would miss him badly and always wish that we might have met under different circumstances, with none of the tensions between us.

By the time I went to bed I had a terrible headache, but there were no tears on my pillow. Tears were pointless when I had made up my mind to leave Huntersmere and all its problems behind me. Tomorrow I would be home, facing the prospect of job-hunting again, getting back into my normal routine and trying to forget that I had left part of myself in darkest Lincolnshire.

In the middle of the night, I was shocked out of sleep by a terrific explosion that rocked the cottage. I was out of bed before I was properly awake. Instinct made me rush for the door, but when I opened it I was met by a blast of heat and fumes and a vivid glare of light. I slammed the door and stood for a moment trying to comprehend. The gas. Of course. Something had happened with the gas. I had to get out.

Already I could hear the roar and crackle of the fire. As I stumbled to the window, I tripped over my case and fell headlong. I was totally disorientated. I fumbled with the locks of my case, snapping them shut, threw up the window and heaved the case out. A swirl of choking smoke eddied into the room. Coughing, I pulled on a sweater and a pair of jeans over my nightdress. The garden was lit by a red glare from below me. Smoke poured from the broken ground-floor window. It tore at my eyes and throat, half-blinding me. Suddenly the ground seemed a long way away. Fear held me where I was.

'Jane!' a voice called from the darkness. 'Jump, Jane!'

The moonlight showed me Ray running toward the gate. He came through the billowing smoke, waving his arms as if he were swimming. 'Jump! I'll catch you!'

CHAPTER NINE

My lungs ached from coughing and tears ran down my cheeks. Somehow I scrambled over the windowsill, balanced on my stomach, and let myself down. The sweat on my hands made them slippery and suddenly I felt myself plunging downwards, dropping through the choking smoke. I fetched up with a thud, knocking Ray over. Both of us went sprawling and for a moment I couldn't breathe.

Then Ray was dragging me to my feet, half carrying me to the gate where I flopped down. Other people were arriving from the village, some of them in dressing gowns. I heard the babble of voices, asking questions, saying the fire brigade was coming. I was too confused to think straight.

Through aching eyes I saw that the ground floor of the cottage was ablaze. Flames licked round the front window; smoke belched up to the moonlit sky like a great brown genie. A woman bent over me, asking if I was all right, then Ray was beside me again, wanting me to move further from the cottage.

A searing pain shot through my foot as I stood up, making me feel faint. Someone carried me across the lane to the soft cool grass beneath the trees, where people gathered round me. They examined my foot with the help of a torch and took out a chunk of glass, from the shattered window. A woman was binding the wound when I heard Joel, his voice almost unrecognisable with fear, shouting, 'Where's Jane? Is Jane out? Where's Jane?'

The group of people parted to allow Joel through and he flung himself down beside me, gathering me into his arms. I clung to him as if he were a lifeline, hearing him gasp for breath, his heart thudding. He had run all the way from Huntersmere.

When the fire engines arrived, the people moved away to watch them pour water on the blaze. I was left alone with Joel, except that Ray hovered nearby. A reporter arrived, and then the police. And all the while the fire hoses fought the dying blaze. My memory of that time is a confusion of flames, smoke, steam,

178

milling people and shouting voices.

Finally, Joel and I were taken back to Huntersmere in a police car. We couldn't use the Mini because its keys were in the cottage, but someone had rescued my battered case, so at least I had a supply of clothes.

The big house was in darkness as Joel helped me up the steps. He said that his mother slept like the dead because she took sleeping pills and Partridge didn't wear his hearing aid at night, so neither of them would be aware of what had happened. We half expected to encounter Irene, but since there was no sign of her we assumed that she had slept through the explosion.

'You may as well sleep in Gareth's room tonight,' Joel said. 'We'll arrange something more permanent in the morning. Can you make it up the stairs?'

I could, though my foot was painful and I was sorry to have to lean on Joel when he was carrying my case. He was even more tired than I was. But eventually we reached Gareth's room and I flopped down on the bed.

'What do you think caused it?' Joel asked. 'Did you leave the gas on?'

'No, I'm sure I didn't. You heard what I told the police. I don't know how it happened.'

He was frowning down at the hands clasped between his knees. 'It's damn peculiar. Even if there was a leak, what made the stuff explode? I thought it must be an aircraft crashing. I

179

couldn't figure out which direction it came from, until I went to the bathroom and saw the fire. But there aren't any naked flames in the cottage. Nothing to cause a spark. It's a hell of a coincidence after all the other peculiar things that have been happening.'

'Joel!' I sat up, horrified. 'You don't think ... Why would anyone want to harm *me*?'

'That's what I'm wondering. I thought it was a freak accident until Prentiss ... Did you hear what he said?'

'About what?'

Joel looked at me with hollow, haunted eyes. 'He asked me if I'd quarrelled with you. That's all he said, but it was enough. After all, if I'm trying to kill Gareth why shouldn't I try to kill you, too?'

There was such weary hopelessness in him that my eyes stung with fresh tears and I put my arms round his neck, holding him close to me. 'Don't talk like that. Please don't. They'll soon find out who's really responsible.'

'Oh, Jane! I was so afraid ...' His fingers twined in my hair, turning my face to his, and his mouth found mine. We kissed with desperate passion, hungrily, achingly. I found myself lying on the bed while his lips pressed on my eyes, my ear, my throat, and finally we lay close together, our limbs entwined as if we would become part of one another, never to be separated. Slowly I felt the tension drain out of him. His muscles relaxed and within a few

180

minutes he was asleep. That was how tired he was. Contented, I burrowed closer to him and myself settled down.

I struggled up through layers of unconsciousness, disturbed by the unusual sensation of another body moving in the bed. I felt Joel get up and as I opened my eyes he switched off the light, leaving only the greyness of early morning in the room.

'Joel?'

'Sssh. Go back to sleep. I'm sorry I woke you.'

I pushed myself up onto my elbows, peering blearily at him. 'Where are you going?'

'To my own room. Forgive me. I never meant... Why don't you get into bed properly? You'll rest better.'

'You don't have to go,' I said.

'Of course I do!' he replied roughly, and went away.

Still half-asleep, I took off my jeans and sweater and climbed between the sheets, but I lay awake for a long time, feeling hurt by the way he had left me and wondering what I had done to annoy him.

Waking for the second time that morning, I was startled to see Partridge standing by the bed.

'It's nearly half past eleven, miss,' he informed me, placing a tray on the bedside table. 'Mrs Ellis is concerned to know how you are this morning. What a terrible thing to

181

happen.'

'Will you tell Mrs Ellis I'm fine, please?' I said. 'I'll be down shortly. Do you know where Mr Ellis is?'

'He may be in the garden, or at the cottage. I'm not sure.'

When he had gone I sat up and drank the coffee he had brought, then ran a hot bath. My foot was very sore but there didn't seem to be any glass left in it. I soaked it until the blood ran again, to make sure it was clean, and bound it with a bandage I had in my case. It was really lucky that I had packed nearly everything.

My stomach hurt a little where I had scraped it on the window-sill and some of my muscles ached, but apart from that—and the fact that I had to walk on the heel of my injured foot—I felt fit enough as I limped across the library and down the stairs.

I could hear Mrs Ellis on the phone in the morning room. When she saw me, she said, 'Oh, here she is now. I'll let you talk to her ... Jane, it's your mother. I thought I'd better call her before she heard it from some other source. The radio and television people have been at the cottage.'

So I talked to Mum, who had just got in from work, and assured her that I was in one piece. Yes, I would see her on Friday evening. I would tell her the whole story then.

'This is a most dreadful thing to have happened,' Mrs Ellis said as I put the receiver down. 'One hears of gas explosions, of course, but I never dreamed it could happen here. My dear ... are you sure you're perfectly well? You could have stayed in bed.'

'I'd rather be up,' I said. 'Do you think I ought to go to the cottage?'

'I wouldn't, if I were you. There may be reporters still about. You don't want to be bothered with them. Some fire investigators are here, too, but if they want to see you they'll come to the house. Joel seems to be coping, though he looks haggard this morning.' Suddenly there were tears in her eyes. 'Everything's going wrong! All the trouble about Gareth, and now this. If only Serena were here!'

'Well, she isn't!' Joel said from the doorway, making us both look round. Haggard was the word for him. There were dark circles under his eyes and his whole face looked drawn, as if he had aged ten years overnight. 'Don't crack up on me, mother.'

She wiped her eyes surreptitiously. 'I won't, dear. I've just been phoning Jane's mother to reassure her. What's happening at the cottage?'

'They say the back window had been forced. The gas taps were all turned on full. It wasn't an accident.'

Mrs Ellis gave a choking gasp, one hand clapped to her mouth. I just stared, stricken, at Joel's grim face. After a moment, he turned on his heel and strode out to the hall.

'Joel!' I went after him. 'Are they sure? But it's crazy! Who would want me dead?'

'I don't know!' he said harshly. 'But whatever your friend Prentiss thinks, it wasn't me!'

'I never thought it was!'

He started up the stairs, paused, and looked at me across the bannister. 'Your car's all packed. Your case was, too. Were you planning on leaving?'

'Yes, I ... thought it might be best.'

'That's a good idea. The sooner, the better!' With that he stamped on up the stairs, leaving me struggling against tears of bewilderment, and as I turned away I saw Irene watching me with an expression of satisfaction. She would be glad to see me leave, too.

When I returned to the morning room, Mrs Ellis was drying more tears with a lace-edged handkerchief. 'I heard what he said. He doesn't mean it, Jane. He's overwrought. Of course you can't leave yet, not while your foot is like that. You couldn't drive.'

'I haven't got the car keys, anyway,' I said with a choked laugh. 'I left them in the kitchen at the cottage. I must ask Mum to bring the spare set when she comes.'

'I've been wondering if I should put her off. I don't know. Perhaps their visit will cheer us all up. We'll decide about that later.'

Her distress and Joel's black mood prevented all but the minimum of conversation at lunch. Soon afterwards, Joel departed to visit Gareth. He didn't ask me to go with him and I hadn't the courage to suggest it. Once again he had gone cold on me, for reasons which I did not understand, not even slightly.

It was while Joel was out that Ray came. Partridge wouldn't let him into the house, so I had to go out to the terrace to talk to him, which didn't please him.

'Joel Ellis must think he's the Lord almighty,' he muttered. 'How are you, Jane? How's the foot?'

'I'll live,' I said. 'And Ray ... thank you for what you did. If you hadn't turned up I might have stood there petrified until it was too late.'

'Well, it's a pity Joel flaming Ellis didn't stay with you again last night, then *he* could have played hero.'

'Joel? Why ... Ray, what do you mean?'

'Oh, don't play the innocent! I know he was with you all Monday night. His car was there when I came out of the "Bull" and it was still there when I went to work the next morning. I know because I looked.'

'But ... Ray, Joel wasn't with me. His car was, I know—because he lent it to me. He was too tired to drive me himself.'

'Oh,' Ray said flatly. 'Then I'm sorry. I was jealous as hell. I imagined he was there again last night. I couldn't sleep for thinking about the two of you, so I got up to stare in that direction and ... boom! Up she went. You do

185

know they're treating it as arson?'

'Yes, Joel told us.'

'Have you made any enemies here?'

'None that I know of, except maybe Irene, but I don't think she hates me enough to want me dead.'

'You didn't quarrel with Joel?'

I was silent for a moment, too angry to speak. 'If you're going to say stupid things like that you might as well leave right now. It was not Joel. It has never been Joel. He's so worried about this whole thing he's nearly out of his mind. Why don't you stop hounding him? Didn't you get enough copy last night?'

'All I got was another puzzle,' Ray said. 'And I'm sorry, but Joel Ellis fits the bill just too perfectly. Motive, opportunity ... For what's happened to Gareth, anyway. The fire I'm not so sure about, unless you quarrelled. Maybe he's got a taste for murder.'

Incensed, I hit him with my clenched fist, catching him full in the chest. There wasn't much power in the blow, but he stepped away and I fled into the house, hating him. How dare he say such things about Joel?

For the second time that day, I came face to face with Irene in the hall.

'More reporters?' she asked. 'Ghouls, they are. You shouldn't talk to them.'

'I shan't any more,' I vowed.

As I went into the sitting room a thought struck me—Irene had been cousin to

Elizabeth. If Gareth died, would Irene have a claim to the Figgins fortune? But when I asked Mrs Ellis she said that Irene and Elizabeth were related through their mothers, so Irene had no Figgins blood in her. Mrs Ellis seemed shocked that I had ever thought of such a thing.

The room next to Mrs Ellis's had been prepared for my use that night. I hardly saw Joel, apart from half an hour over dinner. He said that Gareth was progressing well and expected to be allowed home at the end of the week. The rest of the time he was working, either in the garden or in the study, and it was clear that he was avoiding me.

I cried myself to sleep that night, mostly because Joel had again closed the door on me and this time it was firmly shut, leaving him alone with the worries that were slowly tearing him apart.

By the time I went down the following morning, Joel had already gone out to work. His mother said he had got up early and gone without breakfast. She was extremely worried about him, and so was I although I couldn't say so.

Hoping to catch a glimpse of him, I walked past the greenhouses to the cottage, but there was no sign of Joel. I hoped I might find something salvageable at the cottage, but one look at the blackened, wet interior was enough to put me off. Everything that I had left to pack

187

at the last moment was lost—including my handbag and the car keys. The Mini stood as if abandoned, holding all my books and ornaments. The walk had been a bad idea.

I was turning away from the cottage, depressed, when a car purred to a stop, coming from the village. Seeing me, the driver climbed out and I realised there was something familiar about him, though I couldn't place where I had seen him before. He looked to be around forty, of medium height, fair-haired, wearing a sports shirt and slacks. Everything about him was expensive, from the gold watch on his wrist to the gleaming Mercedes behind him.

'Yes, it's me again,' he said with a wry little smile. 'Were you hurt? You're limping.'

'I ... cut my foot.' I stayed where I was, several yards away. What on earth did he mean—'it's me again'?

'I saw it on the news last night,' he said. 'That's why I came back. There's something odd about everything. Do you know Miss Reid? Miss Irene Reid?'

'Yes,' I said cautiously. 'I'm sorry, but ... should I know you?'

'Last Saturday night. Here in the garden. I scared the wits out of you.'

My mind went blank with shock. My ears roared. The next thing I knew he was beside me, supporting me with his arm and softly cursing himself.

'What a fool I am! After the ordeal you've

been through. Come and sit in the car.'

'No!' I jerked away from him. 'Who are you? What do you want?'

'My name is Andrew Raymond. Does that mean anything to you? ... No, I thought not. Please, don't be afraid of me. I'm on my way to Huntersmere to see whoever's in charge. There's a few things that I want to get straight. Maybe I'm the proverbial fool rushing in, but ... Where are you staying? May I give you a lift?'

'I'm staying at Huntersmere.'

'Then let me take you back, Miss ...'

'Ashborne. Jane Ashborne. Look ... what's this about? What were you doing here on Saturday night?'

'Just looking. Looking at the cottage where my father once lived. I should have stopped to explain, but she's been so adamant about my staying away.'

'She?'

'Miss Reid.'

'I'm afraid I still don't understand,' I said, though my distrust was ebbing away.

'I can hardly expect you to. I'm a ... what you might call a skeleton in the closet. Of the Figgins family. They owned this estate at one time.'

'Yes, I know. You said ... your father lived here? Was he a gardener?'

'I've been told he was a carpenter. His name was Peter Brown.'

I stared at him in disbelief, my mind working. 'Then your mother was...'

'Elizabeth Figgins, of Huntersmere. I was illegitimate, it seems.'

'I think,' I said, 'that we had better go and talk to Joel.'

Andrew Raymond parked his car by the greenhouses and waited while I went to find Joel. By that time he was with the tomatoes again, spraying a fine mist onto the yellow flowers at the top of the plants to set the crop. After one glance at me he continued with the task.

'If you've come to fetch me in for elevenses,' he said flatly, 'you can save your breath. I'm too busy.'

'It's something more important than elevenses,' I replied. 'At least, it seems to be. There's a man outside. His name is Andrew Raymond.'

'I've never heard of him. What is he—police, or media?'

'Neither. Joel, will you please listen! He says ... he says he's Elizabeth Figgins' son.'

Joel whipped round, almost wetting me with the spray. He thrust the container into my hands and pushed past me to stride determinedly towards the door. I followed, leaving the spray on the path, and saw that Andrew Raymond was leaning against his car, totally relaxed, though when he saw Joel he stood up and extended a hand.

'What the devil is this?' Joel demanded. 'Who the hell are you?'

Andrew Raymond thrust the hand into his pocket, one eyebrow lifted. 'My name is Andrew Raymond. I'm a chartered surveyor. From London. I assume you're Joel Ellis.'

'Please, Joel!' I begged, seeing him frown. 'Just listen.'

'I'm listening,' he growled. 'But this had better be good. You claim to be Elizabeth Figgins' son? As far as I'm aware, she only had one, and that was my half-brother David.'

The other man leaned through his car window and took a slim briefcase from the back seat. Opening it, he produced a paper which he handed to Joel without comment. It was a copy of a birth certificate, the mother's name clearly written 'Elizabeth Anne Emily Figgins', with an address in London. It was dated 1938. Joel stared at it as if he didn't believe his eyes.

'I was adopted when I was two weeks old,' Andrew Raymond said. 'My parents have been wonderful, but I've always been intrigued to know who my natural parents were. Under the new law, I was able to obtain that copy. It took a bit of detective work, but early this year I discovered that Elizabeth Figgins lived—or had lived—here at Huntersmere. I wrote to her—or to someone who could tell me where she was.'

Joel's head jerked up. 'I remember the letter.

When we saw it was addressed to Elizabeth we gave it to Irene Reid—she was Elizabeth's cousin. She told us it was from someone doing research for a book.'

'Then I'm afraid she lied,' Andrew Raymond said.

'But ... did she reply to you?'

'We've corresponded several times. Apparently my natural father was a carpenter. He lived in that cottage which has just been burnt out.'

Surprise made Joel silent for a moment, then he said, 'I knew she had an affair with a carpenter, but I never knew there had been a child.'

'No, you wouldn't. According to Miss Reid, only she and Sir George knew that Elizabeth was pregnant. After the elopement was prevented, Elizabeth was sent to London until after she had had me. They gave out that she had been sent away to forget about her lover. By the time she came back, he had gone to the war and Sir George had arranged another bridegroom for her.'

'My father, yes. Then David was born and Elizabeth died.'

'So I've been informed. Even so, I was curious to see the place where they had lived, but Miss Reid kept finding reasons to delay me. There's a furtive element about her letters. The more I've read them, the more they've disturbed me, especially this last few days. Last weekend I was almost passing the doorstep—on my way home from a business conference—so I decided to stay overnight in Lincoln and just take a look. The cottage appeared to be deserted, and my curiosity got the better of me. That, I'm afraid,' with an apologetic glance at me, 'is when I startled Miss Ashborne.'

'Then why on earth didn't you stop to explain? We thought you were a burglar or something.'

'I ought to have done. But at the time I felt so embarrassed ... Miss Reid had written about complications she couldn't go into. I thought I might unwittingly have upset things if I had announced my identity. I telephoned Miss Reid later, to apologise for alarming the young lady and ... well, that's when I started to worry. Miss Reid was furious with me. She sounded almost unbalanced. She said I had "probably ruined everything". That was on Tuesday evening. When I saw on the news that the cottage had gone up in flames only hours later, and arson was suspected ... I talked it over with my wife and we decided I ought to come up here and confess.'

'You've only been here once before?' Joel asked, as if to get it clear in his mind.

'That's right. Just last Saturday night.'

'Does Irene know what you look like?'

'No. We've only been in contact by letters, and that one phone call. Why? I'm sorry, but I

193

fail to see...'

'Oh, you'll see,' Joel assured him. 'You were right to come, Mr Raymond. That fire was the last of a string of peculiar happenings. Will you come up to the house?'

I must admit that I didn't see what connection there might be, but I limped along behind as the two men walked to the house. I sensed a growing excitement in Joel, as if the great weight of tension was beginning to lift.

We gathered with Mrs Ellis in the sitting room and Partridge brought coffee for us all. As the butler was leaving, Joel called him back and asked:

'You were here before the war, weren't you, Partridge? You remember Miss Elizabeth?'

'Oh, very clearly,' the old man said. 'A lovely girl, she was. Beautiful.'

'Do you remember her attempted elopement?'

The butler hesitated, glancing round at us all as if wondering how much he should say.

'It's all right,' Joel said. 'No one here is going to take offence. Tell us what you remember.'

'Well, Mr Ellis... There had been some talk among the staff. We knew that Miss Elizabeth was sneaking off to meet the man. He was staying at the cottage, doing some work on the church for Sir George. Fine young chap, he was. Handsome and well set up. It was no wonder Miss Elizabeth fell for him.'

'What was Miss Reid doing at the time?' Joel

asked. 'Did she know about the affair?'

'Oh, yes. She was Miss Elizabeth's confidante. The maid used to hear them talking. But it was obvious to us that Miss Reid was jealous. She always was jealous of Miss Elizabeth, and if you ask me, Miss Reid had taken a shine to the young chap, too. It was Miss Reid told Sir George they were planning to run away together. After he brought Miss Elizabeth back, I heard him thanking Miss Reid. "You saved her from her own foolishness, Irene," he said. He sent Miss Elizabeth away to some friends in London and the young chap packed his bags and went to join the Army. Broken-hearted, so they say. He was killed in the war, we heard.'

'But by that time Elizabeth had married my father?'

'That's right. Soon as she got back from London. Sir George rushed her into it—begging your pardon, Mrs Ellis, but the Brigadier was twice her age and they weren't suited. When she heard the news about young Peter being killed she just gave up. Faded away.'

'And how did Miss Reid take the news?' Joel asked.

Once again Partridge looked round at the three of us who were listening, but obviously what he saw encouraged him, for he confided, 'She was nearly out of her mind. Blamed herself, you see. If she hadn't told on them,

Miss Elizabeth would have married the young chap and both of them would have survived. If Peter had lived, Miss Reid could probably have put up with him being married to Miss Elizabeth, but as it was she lost him completely. She said to Bess—that was the maid—"It's my fault he's dead. I killed him." She was in a terrible state.'

'Thank you, Partridge,' Joel said. 'You can go now. Will you ask Miss Reid to come to the sitting room, please? And ... don't tell her we've been discussing her.'

'Yes, sir.' Partridge departed, looking puzzled.

'Joel ...' Mrs Ellis ventured. 'What is all this about? You said Mr Raymond was a surveyor. I thought he'd come about the stairs.'

Joel shook his head. 'No, mother. He's the product of Elizabeth's affair with Peter the carpenter, her illegitimate son.'

'Her what?'

'Sssh! Irene will be here any minute. I'll explain it all later.'

He left his seat and was by the door when Irene arrived looking irritated. 'Mrs Ellis, I'm very busy planning menus for the weekend. With your friends coming ...' The sentence trailed off as she stared at Andrew Raymond and behind her Joel closed the door, leaning on it.

'This is Andrew Raymond,' he said. 'You've been corresponding with him, Irene. Aren't you going to say hello?'

Her face went white. She gasped, 'You fool! I told you to stay away until...'

'Until when, Irene?' Joel prompted.

But she had regained control of herself. She walked across to Andrew, holding out a hand that trembled slightly. 'I'm glad to meet you. It was just ... I was afraid Mrs Ellis might be upset if you came. Her husband was once married to Elizabeth, you know.'

'That's rather a feeble excuse,' Joel said. 'Why don't you tell him the truth?'

She hesitated for only a fraction of a second, then gave Andrew a tight smile. 'The truth. Yes. Did I tell you that Elizabeth—your mother—was a very wealthy woman? She left everything she had to David, her son by Brigadier Ellis. But that wasn't right. She had two sons. Half of everything she owned is yours by right.'

Mrs Ellis was staring in horror. 'Irene!'

'This is nonsense!' Andrew exclaimed, his colour rising. 'I've no intention of making any claims. That was never my object. All I ever asked...'

'But it's your right!' Irene cried. 'You belong here. You would have been the heir if I hadn't...'

'I have no place here!' Andrew protested. 'I have parents who raised me. I've a wife and children, a home in London, a good career. I want nothing from Huntersmere!'

Irene grasped his arm with her one good hand, her eyes glittering. 'You *must*! Don't you understand? Everything I've done has been for you. All the risks I've ...' She stopped abruptly, realising what she was saying, and swung round as if to leave, only to find Joel still guarding the door.

'What is she talking about?' Andrew asked in bewilderment.

'She's talking about her attempts at murder,' Joel said, and his voice was hard. 'She loved your father. She was obsessed by him. She stopped him from marrying Elizabeth and because of that he was killed. At least, that's the way she sees it. Because of her, there was nothing left of the man she loved, except for a baby, lost somewhere by adoption. And when you contacted her it must have seemed like a miracle. It gave her a chance to absolve her guilt, to see Peter's son take his rightful place here. But in order to do that she had to dispose of the legitimate heir. Isn't that right, Irene?'

She was staring at him coldly, her whole body stiff. She made no reply.

'She has tried four times to kill Gareth,' Joel said grimly. 'She wanted you, Andrew, to stay away until she had succeeded, so that you wouldn't be implicated in any murder investigation. She planned to see me put in jail for it. Only you spoiled things by turning up at the cottage, by letting Jane see you. Irene was terrified that Jane might recognise you later,

198

and bring suspicion on you. So she tried to kill Jane, too. You bitch, Irene!'

'You can't prove anything,' she said, though her voice trembled. 'I'll deny it. You have absolutely no proof.'

'Motive, means, and opportunity,' Joel said. 'That's what the police look for. We know most of the means and you certainly had the opportunity. This morning you've given us the motive, too. You would have loved to see Peter's son take over here—take over from the Ellises whom you despise. Did you plan to pretend he was *your* son? Is that the fantasy you cherished?'

'He has more right here than you do!' Irene snapped.

'I have *no* right here!' Andrew said, throwing out his hands. 'If you had told me from the beginning, I would have made that clear. Whatever you've done, it has been for nothing. I belong with my real family, not here among strangers.'

Irene stared at him, beginning to sag at the knees. She dropped into a chair, her head in her hands, her shoulders shaking. It was difficult to tell whether she was laughing or crying. Perhaps it was a mixture of both.

'But Joel ...' Mrs Ellis put in breathlessly. 'How could Irene have done all those things? She only has the use of one arm.'

Irene whirled to look at her, eyes full of hatred. 'I can do more with one arm than you

199

can with two, you stupid woman!'

CHAPTER TEN

Irene sat, passive and silent, until the police arrived. Having heard the gist of the story, two of them took her away for questioning while others stayed to interview everyone in the house. They took copious notes before leaving us in peace.

It was surprising how, now that Irene had virtually confessed, people began to remember significant things. Mrs Farrier recalled seeing Irene sneak a kitchen knife into the house, only a few days before the swing rope gave way. Both she and Partridge said that Irene was an expert on herbal medicine, so it followed that she must also know about natural poisons. Didn't the Ellises remember that, on the night of the almost-fatal dinner-party, Mrs Farrier had had to leave early, and Irene had completed preparations for the meal? And Partridge recalled that Irene had herself made Gareth's bedtime drink that evening. Probably, he thought, she had given the boy an extra dose of whatever had made the rest of them ill.

They read new meanings into all of these occurrences, though before they had not suspected anything. After all, no one had guessed that Irene had a motive for murder. No one had known about Andrew.

The innocent cause of it all stayed for a late lunch under gentle duress from Mrs Ellis, though it was clear that he would have preferred to be gone. During the meal Mrs Ellis proved that she, too, could be wise in retrospect.

'Of course,' she said, 'I always knew Irene was a deep one. I never did know what she was thinking. To be honest, I always felt uncomfortable with her. She was so brusque. I thought it was because she felt she was a cut above us—being Elizabeth's cousin, I mean. There were times when I wanted to ask her to leave. But she has been here all her life. This has been her home. I couldn't bring myself to put her out. But to think she was capable of such … It's incredible.'

'It's a good thing Andrew came when he did,' Joel said. 'She might have succeeded next time.'

'Yes,' his mother breathed. 'Oh, it's too awful to think about. Andrew, you must come and see us again, at a happier time. Bring your family. Your children are Gareth's cousins, you know.'

Andrew stared unhappily at his plate. 'I've caused you too much worry and trouble as it is. I'm just a ghost from the past. I know what I wanted to know, but Elizabeth Figgins and Peter Brown are just names. My real parents are John and Ann Raymond. That's one thing I've learned. No, I won't come back. You do understand?'

He didn't linger when the meal was finished. Joel went to see him off, while Mrs Ellis and I watched from the open french window in the sitting room, seeing the Mercedes glide down the drive, taking Andrew Raymond out of our lives. Poor man, I think he was sorry he had started out on his quest to trace his origins.

Joel came slowly back up the steps. The burden had gone from his shoulders but it had left him drained. He hadn't looked at me directly for hours, almost ignoring me, and I myself felt empty, unable even to be glad that the mystery was finally solved.

'It's too late now to go and see Gareth,' he said with a glance at his watch. 'I'll leave it until tonight.'

'Well, I hope you're not intending to go back to work,' his mother said. 'You look worn out. Why don't you go and have a rest? That's what I'm going to do. All this upset has tired me out. I'll see you later, Jane.'

I watched her move painfully to the door, supported by her stick, and I was aware of Joel only two feet away physically, though there were miles between us in every other way.

'Are you still planning to leave?' he asked.

'There's no reason for me to stay. Gareth won't be fit enough for lessons for a while and, if you want my opinion, he's only been getting

202

low marks this last term because he's been worrying. Now that it's all over he'll be able to concentrate again. Let him have his holiday.'

'When will you go?'

'With my parents on Sunday.'

'You must wish you'd never come here.'

I couldn't look at him, so I stared out over the park. 'It's been an experience, anyway. Never a dull moment since I arrived.'

There was a long moment of silence before Joel said, 'I think I'll take mother's advice and get some rest,' and I waited with my eyes fixed on the distant gateway until I heard the door close.

The scene began to dance and dazzle before my eyes. Slow tears dripped down my cheeks. Knowing only that I had to be doing something, I stepped out onto the terrace and limped down the steps. Ray's prediction had been true. Joel had used me, even made use of my love for him when he needed comfort, and now I was to be allowed to go, to walk away from this place and these people who had become almost as close as my own family.

I followed the drive for a short distance, then cut across the lawn to the woods and the sanctuary of the sun-dappled shade there. Like a wounded animal I curled up in the long grass beneath a tree and sobbed until my face was streaming and my body aching with misery.

A twig cracked close beside me and I froze. From somewhere above me, Joel said, 'Janie?

Janie, why are you crying?'

I couldn't answer. I lay with my clenched fist against my mouth, stiffening when his hand came on my shoulder.

He sat down beside me, saying quietly, 'Are you as unhappy as I am?'

'What are you unhappy for?' I muttered. 'Everything's fine now. You can explain to Gareth. He'll understand. Then you can carve another notch on your hunting knife and go looking for the next idiotic female that...'

He pulled me forcibly onto my back, bending over me, his hands pinning me to the ground. 'Don't say that! It's not true!'

'Isn't it?' I raged. 'Don't you dare pretend you care about me. If you did, you wouldn't have treated me the way you have. You've just made use of me.'

'I haven't! I swear to you ... Jane, I was confused after the fire. You seemed to be in danger because of me. I wanted you to go home, where you would be safe, even if I had to hurt you.'

'But you've done it before,' I reminded him, unable to see him for tears. 'Blowing hot and cold all the time. I've never known where I was with you.'

'Don't you know why I blew hot and cold?' Joel asked desperately. 'Good grief, I had a charge of attempted murder hanging over me. How could I drag you into that? But there were times when I needed you so much I couldn't

204

help myself. I wished I could keep running to you the way Gareth did, but I couldn't. It wouldn't have been fair.'

Blinking, I saw how wretched he looked, but before I could say anything he had turned away, his back to me. 'It's too late for excuses, I know. I've hurt you too much. I destroy every relationship with my foul moods. But this is the first time it's hurt so bloody much.'

'Joel,' I managed, running my hand up his back. 'I thought you were going to rest.'

'How can I rest when . . .' He swung round to look at me. 'Is it too late? Will you forgive me?'

'Only if you forgive me,' I said, and held out my arms to him.

'Oh, Jane!' he breathed, and came to me, his mouth seeking mine feverishly. We kissed until we were breathless, our bodies fitting together as if they had been made for that purpose.

'Oh, I love you,' he murmured, laying his head on my breast, one hand still tangled in my hair. 'I love you, Janie.'

'And I love you,' I whispered, rejoicing in the strength of his body against mine, the muscles beneath his shirt, his hair like warm silk to my touch.

We lay there without speaking and I felt him slowly relax. For the second time he went to sleep in my arms, there with the sheltering leaves above us. Closing my eyes, I let all my senses concentrate on him, glad that he found comfort with me, and after a while everything faded and I, too, slept.

When I woke the sun had moved round and was pouring in long golden streams through the trees. Joel was still asleep, but stirred when I breathed his name.

'You'll have to move,' I murmured. 'My arm's asleep.'

He opened his eyes, blue and languorous, and gave me a sleepy smile. 'I was dreaming about you.'

'Good. Joel, love, you're on my arm!'

He shifted so that my arm came free, then bent over me and kissed me deeply. 'I love you. Did I tell you that?'

'Several times. Do you remember that I said I love you, too?'

He smiled into my eyes. 'How could I forget? You can say it as often as you like. I'll never get tired of hearing it.'

Reaching up, I pulled his head down and kissed him, unable to have enough of him.

'You should be careful,' he said in a low voice. 'I'm not so tired any more.'

'I'm glad,' I said with a laugh. 'If you go to sleep on me again I might begin to think I bore you.'

'You tempt me to prove that a lie,' he said. 'But we'd better move. The ground's getting damp.' That seemed to remind him of the passage of time and he glanced at his watch, sitting up with a jerk. 'Lord! It's nearly dinnertime. Mother will be wondering where we are. Come on. Up!'

He pulled me to my feet and led me through the trees, pausing to say, 'Will you come with me to the hospital? Gareth might believe the story of today's events if you tell him.'

'He'll believe you, too. But I'll come if you want me to.'

Joel gave me a wry little smile. 'You did say you were sick of being my go-between.'

'I know, but ... I was angry.'

'Yes,' he agreed affably. 'You have got quite a temper when you get going.'

'The pot calling the kettle?' I teased. 'Anyway, when you're the youngest of four children you sometimes have to raise your voice to be heard above the din. That's my excuse.'

Laughing, Joel kissed me and we walked on towards Huntersmere.

Arriving at the hospital that evening, we found Gareth out of bed, wrapped in a dressing gown at a table in the solarium, busy making his model ship. He saw that Joel's hand was around mine and his look became questioning.

'Should you be doing that with a dislocated shoulder?' I asked.

'It's a bit stiff, but they told me I could use my arm. Are you all right? Joel told me about the fire.'

'Yes, I'm fine, thank you. Stepped on a piece of glass, but nothing worse.' I dropped into a chair beside him while Joel walked round to sit on the end of the table on Gareth's other side. Gareth shot him an uncertain look before turning back to me.

'I can come home tomorrow. In the morning. Will you come and fetch me?'

'Of course we will,' I said. 'It will be nice to have you home. We really miss you. Don't we, Joel?'

'Like you'd miss a headache,' Joel said drily, and tousled the boy's hair. Gareth stiffened, but he didn't draw away.

'Shall we tell him about all the excitement he's missed?' Joel asked, glancing round the solarium. The only other people there were a patient and his wife at the far end of the room.

'What excitement?' Gareth said suspiciously.

'The police have made an arrest,' Joel told him. 'They've found the person who was responsible for all your "accidents"—and for causing that fire.'

Gareth turned to me for confirmation. 'Have they? Who is it?'

'Irene,' I told him.

The explanations took most of the visiting hour. Gareth knew all about people having affairs and illegitimate babies and he wasn't at all perturbed by that aspect, but he found it more difficult to grasp the idea of an obsessive, unrequited love that stretched to the loved one's child, too. In the end, however, he wasn't so much interested in the reasons for Irene's

208

crimes as the fact that she had done them.

When the telling was done, he was silent for a long time, thoughts racing behind his bright grey eyes; then he turned to Joel, saying, 'But it was Irene who kept telling me it was *you*. She said you needed money and that was the only way you could get it. I thought she was on my side. I thought she was my friend!' He jumped out of his seat, fists clenched, and added fiercely, 'I hope they hang her!'

When the bell rang to signal the end of visiting time, he walked with us to the door of the ward, where he stuck out his hand awkwardly to Joel. It was his way of trying to show that he was sorry, but at least it was a start.

In the car, Joel did not switch on the engine immediately, but sat back with his hands braced against the wheel, heaving a great sigh. 'Thank God for that. I really believe it may work out. And it's all thanks to you, my darling go-between. What would we do without you?'

'Well, you don't need me any more now,' I said, and saw the look he shot me. 'I mean, as a mediator.'

'You mean I don't need to be jealous any more?' He turned in his seat, stroking my face. 'Janie, darling, you misunderstood me the other day. I suspect you did it deliberately, but we'll let that pass for now. You want me to say it?—I wasn't jealous of his affection for you, I was jealous of your affection for him. You held him and kissed him, you even called him "darling", and there was I starving for all those things from you, pining for some sign that you cared.'

'Well, stop pining,' I said, leaning across to kiss him. 'I care, more than you'll ever know.'

The Friday of that week was an exciting day. In the morning we brought Gareth home and watched him open his belated birthday presents, then I was busy about the house helping with the preparations for the arrival of my parents. Mrs Ellis hobbled about with her stick, checking and rechecking everything until I wondered if she was as nervous about the visit as my parents must be.

They had said they would stop and have a meal somewhere on the journey, so we had dinner and then settled down to wait. It was a beautiful evening, the sunset throwing scarlet banners across the sky, and Joel and I leaned on the terrace balustrade to watch Gareth flying a balsa-wood 'plane that had been among his presents. We were talking softly so that our voices didn't carry into the sitting room where Mrs Ellis was relaxing, and neither of us noticed that Gareth had slipped away until he suddenly appeared on the terrace beside us.

'Here,' he said, and thrust something at Joel.

Joel looked in surprise at the object in his hand. It was the key to Gareth's garage, where he kept his motor-bike.

'I won't ride the bike any more until you say I can,' Gareth mumbled, looking at his shoes. 'You keep the key.'

He was saying that he trusted Joel, I realised. Through a mist of tears, I saw that Joel's face was taut with emotion.

'That's okay,' he said huskily. 'You can have the key. You can ride the bike whenever you want, as long as you promise me to be careful and always wear your helmet.'

Gareth lifted his head, eyes wondering. 'You mean it?'

'I mean it.'

'Oh, thanks, Joel! Thanks!' Impulsively, the boy hugged his uncle and darted away into the sitting room, where I heard Mrs Ellis say, 'Don't rush about so, Gareth. It's time you were in bed.'

'I'm staying up to meet Mr and Mrs Ashborne!' he protested.

'Very well. But sit down and wait quietly. You've only just come out of hospital.'

Joel and I exchanged a smile, then he laid an arm about my shoulders and drew me away, to the far end of the terrace. 'Look, Jane. I told you it was spectacular at night.'

In the purple gloaming, lights gleamed from nearby villages. A line of bright orange dots glowed along the ridge and another described the curve of the route from Newark, both lines converging towards the point where on the horizon the cathedral was floodlit, hanging like a jewel between the dark shapes of two trees.

'It's beautiful,' I breathed.

'Yes, I've always thought so. But it's even better now you're here to share it with me. Jane ... Will you marry me?'

I closed my eyes tightly, too choked to speak, my head spinning with joy.

'Did you hear what I said?' Joel asked.

'Oh ... yes. Yes and yes and yes!' I lifted my lips to his and for a long time we were oblivious to everything else in the world, until the sound of a car came from the gateway and we looked to see its headlights pointing down the drive.

'They're here!' I gasped.

'Do you think they'll approve?'

I looked at him in the twilight, laughing. 'Oh, yes. Except that I'm going to have some explaining to do. Three weeks ago I told them you were a bully. I said I didn't even like you. And Dad ...' The memory made me fill up with mirth. 'Dad told me not to get involved. They're going to have a bit of a surprise. Let's go and meet them. I can't wait to show you off.'

212